THE
SIN
BEARER

THE SIN BEARER

A NOVEL BY

Tom Taylor

WORD BOOKS
PUBLISHER
WACO, TEXAS

A DIVISION OF
WORD. INCORPORATED

Scripture quotations in this book concerning the shipwreck described in the Book of Acts (27:1–28:11) are from *The Holy Bible: New International Version*, Copyright © 1973, 1978, International Bible Society. Used by permission of Zondervan Bible Publishers.

Scripture quotations on pp. 88, 103, and 142 are from the King James Version of the Bible.

All other Scripture quotations are from *The New American Standard Bible,* © The Lockman Foundation 1960, 1962, 1971, 1972, 1973, 1975, 1977.

Library of Congress Cataloging in Publication Data:

Taylor, Tom, 1944–
  The sin bearer.

  1. Paul, the Apostle, Saint—Fiction. I. Title.
PS3570.A956S5   1986   813'.54   86-24715
ISBN 0-8499-0573-7

Printed in the United States of America

6 7 8 9 8   BKC   9 8 7 6 5 4 3 2 1

There are three things which are too wonderful for me,
Four which I do not understand:
The way of an eagle in the sky,
The way of a serpent on a rock,
The way of a ship in the middle of the sea,
And the way of a man with a maid.

Proverbs 30: 18, 19

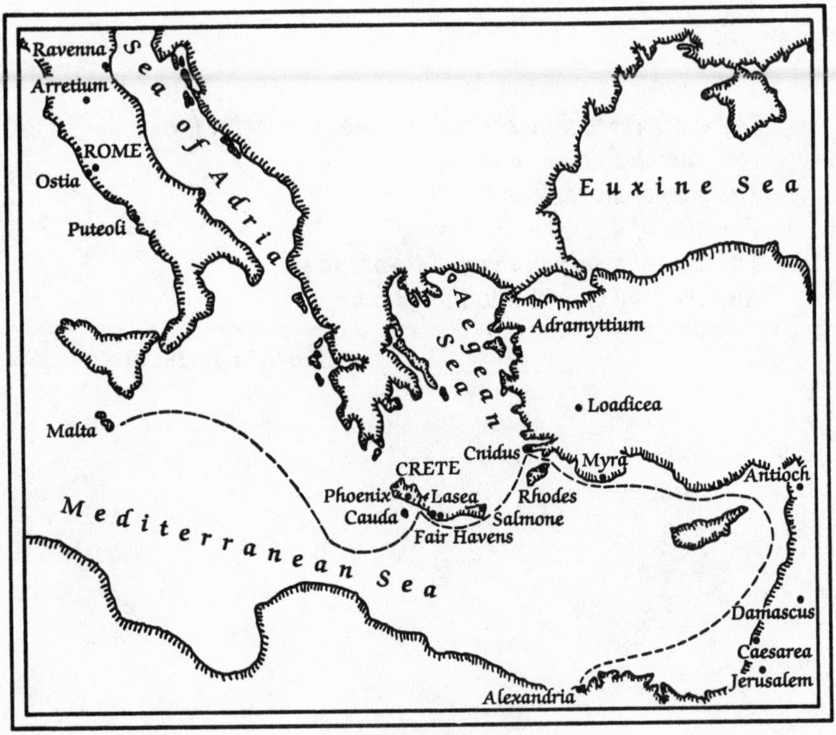
Ravenna
Arretium
ROME
Ostia
Puteoli
Sea of Adria
Euxine Sea
Aegean Sea
Adramyttium
Loadicea
Malta
Cnidus
Myra
CRETE
Antioch
Phoenix
Lasea
Rhodes
Cauda
Salmone
Fair Havens
Mediterranean Sea
Damascus
Caesarea
Jerusalem
Alexandria

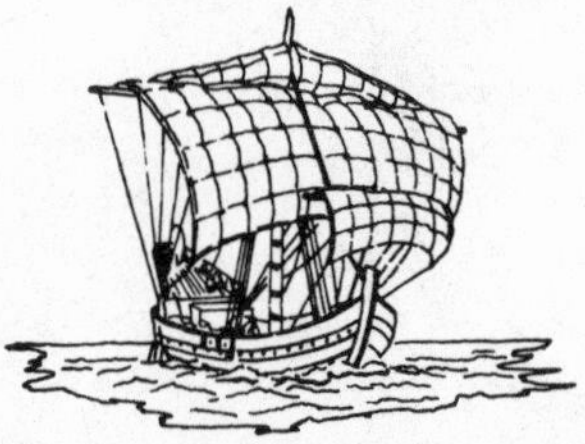

The Voyage of The Athelia

THE
SIN
BEARER

*T*HE WATER GLOWED luminous blue as the young diver began his descent amid a swirling cloud of bubbles. But gradually the blue light faded as he kicked deeper into a graying world on what was intended to be his last dive of the day.

Robert Bonn, an archeology student, had spent most of his summer doing this very thing off the Mediterranean island of Malta. For as long as anyone could remember, fishermen in the area had brought up pieces of ancient jars and bronze artifacts—even a Roman coin dated during the reign of Claudius. All these finds suggested that somewhere in the area was the wreckage of a first-century ship, and the university archeology team had come to Malta on the scent of that tantalizing possibility.

In a summer of searching, Bonn and his fellow team members had charted several significant finds: some gracefully shaped wine jars, the bronze straps of a Roman breastplate, and a bronze lamp. But there had been no hint of the elusive vessel which must have carried those objects. It seemed the *real* beneficiary of their summer's work was Fabio, the grizzled owner of their workboat, the *Falcone*. He and his sons had spent the easiest summer of their lives tending this team of strange scholars who could become so excited over pieces of old jars.

On this dive, however, Bonn was not searching for things ancient. Something was fouling the anchor of the *Falcone*, and he followed the cable downward to discover the problem. In the murky light of the sea bottom he found it. Something which looked like a badly rotted wooden pole had snagged the flukes and prevented them from pivoting out. The anchor had cut deep furrows through the sand and, in the process, had uncovered something—Bonn squinted at what appeared to be a large spear point protruding from the sea bed.

With a tinge of excitement the young archeologist swam instinctively to it. With eyes intent behind his mask, he began gently to brush sand from around the encrusted piece of metal. . . .

From the *Falcone*'s rail they saw his marker buoy pop to the surface. Fifteen minutes later, Bonn himself was back at the boarding ladder and calling for Professor Healey, the team chief.

"An anchor!" Bonn shouted. "I'm sure it is! It has a metal tip, but the fluke is made of wood. When's the last time they used anchors with wooden flukes?"

"Early Christian era?" Healey straightened abruptly and knocked the ashes from his pipe. "I'll suit up. We'll have a look."

"And bring a light," said Bonn. "It's getting dark down there."

Soon Bonn, Healey, and a third member of the team, Karen Chrisman, were floating downward ghostlike through the gloom. Knowing they must leave their find where it lay for the night, they were reluctant to expose much of the ancient wood. But while Karen, her blonde hair waving in the currents, photographed the site, they removed enough silt to discern the distinctive tulip shape of the great wooden fluke. Then they ascended in timed stages toward the throbbing of the *Falcone*'s diesel. Breaking water, Healey grabbed the boarding ladder and spit out his mouthpiece. "It could be first century," he gasped. "It has to be! Bonn, if that anchor went down with the ship, I'd say we've found our wreck!"

The next day was spent in carefully uncovering the old anchor and buoying it in several large pieces to the surface. In itself a priceless find, the anchor also indicated by its sheer size that the ship must have been a large one, probably a merchantman. And so they began searching for the remains of her. With a giant vacuum hose, fed by compressed air pumped down from the *Falcone,* the team began to suck away tons of sand and silt. They worked in widening circles from where the anchor had lain, hoping to uncover an old rib or timber or bronze nails lying in a pattern—anything to indicate the presence of the ship. They searched for days, raising clouds of silt and terrorizing the local octopus population, but of the ship they found absolutely nothing. At last a discouraged Healey conceded defeat. The anchor had obviously been lying alone; it had not gone down with the ship.

"So what do you suppose is most likely?" Bonn asked that evening. "Did the ship sink while lying at anchor? If so, it would have to be somewhere within a close radius."

They sat at their usual table beneath the trees on the cobblestone plaza of the village inn—a dispirited group indeed. Adding to their gloom was the weather forecast which called for a storm to roll in that evening—the first sirocco of autumn—which would stop their work for days. The night was hot with an ominous stillness. Yet the fragrance of gardenias was in the air, and the candles at the restaurant tables flickered like fireflies.

"It's just like a midsummer night," Karen Chrisman mused. "Oberon's night. It's alive somehow . . . You know, I wish it *was* midsummer again, and we had more time."

"More time." Healey growled and rubbed his red-rimmed eyes, then turned to answer Robert's question.

"I don't know, Bonn. The possibilities are endless. The ship *could* have sunk nearby while lying at anchor. Then again, first-century ships carried six anchors or more; a ship might have lost this one and simply sailed on without it. Who knows? *Or* the ship could have anchored offshore in a storm like the one coming in tonight. Her anchor lines broke, and she foundered. That would put the actual wreck site somewhere closer inland."

At that, Bonn sat up erect. "Of course! We should have thought of that possibility first. The anchor *was* lying not far from St. Paul's Bay!"

They looked at him curiously.

"Come on, people. Fabio or anyone else on Malta will tell you that is the place where St. Paul was shipwrecked two thousand years ago. The Bible describes just that type of wreck. The ship was anchored offshore in a storm. When they tried to beach her, they foundered." His eyes swept the group. "Now get this. When they tried to beach the ship, they cut their lines and left their anchors in the sea!"

Karen's eyes widened a bit, and Cal George, the group's antiquities expert, sat up with new interest. "Now that you mention it . . . where *is* that in the Bible?"

Bonn had already pulled out the small New Testament he usually carried and, holding it close to the candle glass, leafed through the pages. "Okay . . . here it is. It's in the Book of Acts—chapter twenty-seven." He glanced at Healey. "Have you heard of it, sir?"

"Oh yes. I am familiar with that chapter of the Acts."

Bonn was mildly surprised, knowing Healey to be an avowed atheist.

"Certainly," said the professor. "I'm sure the narrative includes a great deal of fantasy. Still, it's one of the oldest shipwreck accounts in existence. It tells us a great deal about shipping during that period."

"Well," Bonn's voice tightened at the audacity of what he was going to suggest. "What if our anchor is from that wreck?"

Cal interrupted. "Refresh our memories first, Robert. What does the chapter say?"

His face glowing yellow in the flickering light, Robert quickly scanned the narrative. "Okay," he paraphrased, "the apostle Paul was in Caesarea, and had to go to Rome for trial. He was given to a Roman centurion named Julius, along with some other prisoners. They sailed along the coast in one ship. Then, in the port of Myra, they found another ship—from Alexandria—which was going to Rome."

"From Alexandria?" Cal interrupted thoughtfully. "That means the captain, or the shipowner, was probably Jewish."

"How so?" asked Healey.

"Because in Alexandria at that time there was a large colony of Jews who engaged in shipping Egyptian grain to

Rome. Likely the captain was a very devout Jew." With that, Cal chuckled suddenly. "In that case he probably despised Paul for being a Christian. And he probably hated the Roman centurion too. Lots of conflicts on that voyage, I'd say."

"That's right," mused Robert. "The Romans ruled over the Jews at that time, didn't they?"

"Sure. Just like they did the entire civilized world." Cal paused to figure a moment. "It couldn't have been long after that voyage that the war between Rome and Judea broke out."

Robert's eyes lit in recognition. "That's right! That's when the Romans sacked Jerusalem and scattered the Jews for the last time. They never went back again—at least not until 1948."

"Right. That colony of Jewish shipmen in Alexandria was decimated too. So I guess, whether he lost his ship or not, our captain was living close to the end of his world."

At that, Healey arched his eyebrows and held up his week-old newspaper with headlines of new Russian missiles in Eastern Europe. "Just the same as we are, eh?"

The wry comment left Karen irritated. She tossed her hair back. "Why *must* we always drag in that stuff? I'd like to forget it just for a while."

"Okay, my apologies, Karen. Robert, maybe you should tell us the rest of it. I believe we all prefer the ancient world to this one, anyway."

Cal laughed, and they looked to Robert to continue. But after scanning the chapter for a moment, he frowned. "Too complicated," he muttered. "Why don't I just read it directly. I'll start with the seventh verse."

> We made slow headway for many days and had difficulty arriving off Cnidus. When the wind did not allow us to hold our course, we sailed to the lee of Crete, opposite Salmone. We moved along the coast with difficulty and came to a place called Fair Havens, near the town of Lasea.
>
> Much time had been lost, and sailing had already become dangerous because by now it was after the Fast. So Paul warned them, "Men, I can see that our voyage is

going to be disastrous and bring great loss to ship and cargo, and to our own lives also." But the centurion, instead of listening to what Paul said, followed the advice of the pilot and of the owner of the ship. Since the harbor was unsuitable to winter in, the majority decided that we should sail on, hoping to reach Phoenix and winter there. This was a harbor in Crete, facing both southwest and northwest.

When a gentle south wind began to blow, they thought they had obtained what they wanted; so they weighed anchor and sailed along the shore of Crete. Before very long, a wind of hurricane force, called the "Northeaster," swept down from the island. The ship was caught by the storm and could not head into the wind; so we gave way to it and were driven along. As we passed to the lee of a small island called Cauda, we were hardly able to make the lifeboat secure. When the men had hoisted it aboard, they passed ropes under the ship itself to hold it together. Fearing that they would run aground on the sandbars of Syrtis, they lowered the sea anchor and let the ship be driven along. We took such a violent battering from the storm that the next day they began to throw the cargo overboard. On the third day, they threw the ship's tackle overboard with their own hands. When neither sun nor stars appeared for many days and the storm continued raging, we finally gave up all hope of being saved.

"And so," Bonn went on, "it was probably a storm like the one that's supposed to blow in here tonight, because the ship finally blew here, into Malta. They anchored offshore until daylight, then cut the anchors loose and tried to beach her. But . . . verse forty-one says they didn't make it."

"What happened?" Karen asked.

Robert grinned mischievously. "Why don't you read it yourself?"

"Come on, Bonn! I've never read the Bible in my life. What happened?"

"Read it yourself." He ducked back as Karen took a playful slap at him. "All right. Just for that, the only thing I'll tell you is there were two hundred and seventy-six people aboard."

"And that's probably a lie!"

Bonn was suddenly serious. "No. The Bible gives that figure, Karen—in verse thirty-seven."

"But those ships weren't that big."

Bonn looked questioningly at Cal, who shrugged. "Sorry to disappoint you, Karen, but we have references to ancient ships much bigger than that, actually. We know of one named the *Syracuse* which was designed by Archimedes. It could carry over six hundred passengers in addition to about nineteen hundred tons of cargo. It had three deck levels, passenger cabins, a library and gymnasium. And then, Lucian described a ship named the *Isis* which was one hundred eighty feet long with a beam of forty-five feet. So . . . the ships of that day may have been fatally clumsy during bad weather, but they weren't all small or primitive." Cal glanced at Healey. "I don't suppose ships of equal size were built again until the seventeenth century, were they, Nick?"

"At least," said the Professor. "No, I have no problem with the figure of two hundred seventy-six passengers." He chuckled as he relit his pipe, the flame reflecting on his glasses. "I *do* question other parts of the account, of course. I reject out of hand that God warned St. Paul, or whatever. And there are some other things which don't quite add up."

"Oh? For instance?" said Bonn.

Healey strained for something quickly. "For one thing, no captain of that day in his right mind would have crossed the open sea to Crete during that time of the year, especially if he was a devout Jew who, I assume, would feel some moral responsibility for his passengers. The logical thing is they probably wintered at Cnidus where they would have had everything available to them. Wouldn't that make more sense? Uh, the storm likely occurred when they left Cnidus too early in the spring. So Luke, in his process of deifying St. Paul, was probably covering for the ship's captain, too."

Bonn grimaced in irritation. Many such arguments with Healey had convinced him of their futility. "I don't know," he said. "I'm sure there were good reasons for their crossing to Crete and pressing on, but I can't know what they were."

"And neither, I'm sure, can I." Healey yawned and stretched. "Anybody who wants a ride back to Fabio's can come now—or walk later." And most of the team, drained by the excitement of the day, stood with him as he rose to go.

Robert Bonn couldn't sleep that night. Finally he got up and dressed, and tiptoed down the steps from the garage apartment where he and Cal roomed. Quietly he went out to the storage shed to look again at his anchor.

The pieces of it lay completely covered with sea water in a square shallow tank. The ancient wood would crumble quickly if it were exposed to air, so until the flukes and shaft could be simmered and sealed in a Carbowax compound, the anchor would have to remain submerged. In fascination, Bonn reached into the water and ran his fingers along the eroded wood grain while light from the overhead bulb shimmered on the surface of the tank. What *was* it about the quaint tulip shape of the wooden flukes that so evoked an era of wooden hulls and clumsy, square mainsails? Was it possible this anchor was from the very ship which had wrecked with the apostle Paul? The hair rose on the back of his neck. In the silence, he took his New Testament and began to read again the account of the wreck.

Then the shed door creaked, and he turned to see Karen Chrisman shouldering through the door with two steaming cups in her hands. "Well, what's this?" he said.

"Coffee," she said brightly. "I do this when I can't sleep; and I saw the light out here." She handed him a cup. "So now you can be sleepless the rest of the night. Did you come out here to admire the famous Bonn Anchor? Or are you trying to convince yourself it's real?"

"Both," he said. "I don't know, Karen. Ever since I realized what this anchor could be, the idea has simply captured me."

"Because it's such a direct link?" she ventured.

"I guess that's it. Because the ancient world has so totally passed away, hasn't it? All those people, all that commerce and noise and war—gone as if they never existed. We have some of their writings and a few of their buildings still standing, but they are not real to us. They're just stone figures in a bas-relief carving."

"That's true," she said.

"And then you find something like this—not a stone carving or piece of pottery, but wood!" Affectionately he reached into the tank again. "The apostle Paul could have laid his hand right where mine is now, and admired the workmanship. It was new then, probably varnished with fish oil."

He paused to sip the fragrant coffee, a luxury in Fabio's house where the staple drink was spiced tea.

"Keep going, Bob," Karen said after a moment. "It's fascinating. I mean there is something so *neat* about this night. Maybe it's the storm coming—electricity in the air." She looked down at the anchor. "And we're both so drawn to this thing, aren't we?"

"I can't get those people out of my mind," said Robert simply. "I wonder who the shipmaster was; and if he was really a devout Jew like Cal says. I wonder about the centurion and the others. What were their situations, their plans? What dreams were left in the sea with this anchor?"

With the movement of Bonn's hand the water rippled. In the dancing reflected light the anchor seemed to shimmer and move—as if trying to return to those days when it hung proudly new aboard the thousand-ton freighter *Athelia* . . .

CHAPTER 2

*T*HROUGH THE BRIGHT BLAZING DAYS of mid-autumn they sailed westward. In the shadow of the rigging, young ship-master Abiel Ben Heled leaned to the rudder bars and, by observing the mast's shadow across a bronze ring at its base, held his ship on her heading. The enchantment of sky and sea fell upon him. *Athelia* leaned into the wind as they ghosted along under the huge square mainsail, the topsails and fore-sail all billowing white above them like benign clouds. The gurgle of water aft, the hum of the rigging, the talking and laughter of the passengers—all seemed muted in the sun and without echo, as if sound itself evaporated in the burning blue sky. The crew succumbed to the spell, Abiel knew; and those passengers who still had any life in their souls.

"For a time at least," Abiel thought, "I am as God created me to be." It was an illusion, however vague, of freedom in a world where men were bought and sold like cattle, and where they died in arenas for the pleasure of others.

So benign and harmless was the sea, so heady was the illusion of freedom that it was easy for Abiel to forget the warning once given by his chief financial backer, his fa-ther: "My son, those who sleep in death beneath the waves are those who forgot their fear of the sea. For the sea, like Jehovah, is jealous and will not be mocked."

That afternoon the coast of Lycia rose on the port quarter. Mid-morning of the next day, the *Athelia* glided in bright sunlight through the breakwater of the port of Myra. Abiel had passengers to discharge there; if the price was right, he would also purchase a cargo of wine jars. Far away on the skyline, merchants' houses gleamed in coats of white gypsum. Down closer to the piers were inns, taverns, long warehouses—and stock pens. Once *Athelia* was in the harbor, Calliades of Rhodes, the ship's dour sailmaster, roused himself from the hammock in his cabin and came sleepily to the aft deck to take the helm as required by law. "No need to rouse me, Captain," he growled. "One whiff through the porthole and I knew indeed where we were this blessed hour."

"Don't we all." Abiel grinned laconically as he surrendered the rudder bars to his sailmaster. Then he leaned against the aft deck railing, since there was nothing he need do now except monitor the performance of Calliades and the crew. The land revolved slowly as the ship began a turn to bring the wind, which had been behind them, to a point across the beam. Below on the main deck, sweating bearded seamen in their standard black tunics growled at the passengers to get out of the way as they pivoted the huge mainsail. With rhythmic chants of "Mash-Kou-ha!" they strained against the esparto ropes stretched tight enough to feel like bronze in their calloused hands. A command from the first mate, and several seamen scurried up the mast ladder to fist in the topsails.

A crowd began forming at the small and faraway dock. There would be relatives hoping some long-awaited loved one might be among the passengers on this anonymous ship. There would be the usual shipping agents and speculators. And there would be compliments, Abiel knew, for his ship. The *Athelia*, as beautiful as her name, was one hundred sixty feet long and gracefully formed, with a sharp prow. Over her hull planks was a smooth coating of blue wax, which blended perfectly with the billowing white sails now being furled by seamen small and high on the yardarm.

Sometimes Abiel had to remind himself this ship was really his own. She was truly his love—now, unfortunately, his only love—and the young shipmaster smiled sadly.

Abiel Ben Heled was a tall man, and lean, with large hands

and long, molded bronzed arms. He was not heavily muscled; his great strength seemed to lay in the corded sinews and long, easy sweep of his moves. His dark hair was closely cut at the nape of the neck. With a deep, sonorous voice, black beard, and gaunt face, Abiel could be formidable. New crewmen were always wary of him until they had served long enough to see his deep-set eyes crinkle with humor and acceptance and see he was not so much severe as simply melancholy. Then it was with a bit of affection that they joined the rest of the crew in calling him "the rabbi" behind his back.

Gliding through the smooth water, Calliades steered clear of a harbor boat, its decks stacked with timber. Closer and closer they drew to the dock, as several excited passengers began shouting across the water. Still Calliades, a master at judging wind, current, and momentum, left the mainsail full. Abiel said nothing, trusting him completely. The position of the sailmaster was unique in Roman maritime law. Any time a merchant ship moved under sail, a certified "gubernator," or sailmaster, such as Calliades must be aboard; otherwise, the owner was liable for any damages to passengers and cargo, regardless of the cause. The sailmaster was also second in command of the ship and must take the captain's place should he become disabled at sea. Abiel knew that Calliades lived in dread of this ever happening; at sea he continually watched his captain's health.

At last, at Calliades' command, the crew fanned out in a line across the lower deck and hauled in the brail lines which pulled the mainsail in folds up to the yardarm, spilling the wind. At the same time, seamen on the foredeck let the foresail luff to the breeze. Without power now, the ship drifted on, carried by her great weight. As the stevedores at the dock nervously watched her towering approach, she drifted up past the slip. Ever so slowly she came to a stop, then after several moments began to drift backward with the wind.

"Stand by," Calliades called. Two anchors splashed down from the stern, then two from the bow, and soon the ship was motionless and straining against her anchor lines—not only a mere twenty feet from the dock, but in perfect alignment with it. Good afternoon to the port of Myra.

Abiel smiled, satisfied, for the crowd had seen how a ship from Alexandria conducts herself. There was no need for a boat to come out and tow the *Athelia*'s lines ashore. They were close enough to throw them down to the waiting stevedores who hauled the ship slowly and majestically into her berth. The gangplank went down, and Abiel sighed. Gone was the freedom of the sea and wind. Once again they were part of the devious and enslaved land.

A further reminder of troubled times came later that afternoon in the form of a Roman centurion who, accompanied by his "optio" (sergeant), strode out the pier toward *Athelia*. They paused a moment in terse conference, then ascended the gangplank together, their chest plates and helmets gleaming in the late sun. Many were the respectful nods from the spectators lining the rail. Abiel watched them come, wondering what could be their interest in *Athelia*. The centurion wore the insignia of a "primipilus," meaning he was chief centurion of his legion, a rank, Abiel knew, won only through leadership in combat. He also held the order of "Hasta Pura," the Silver Spear. A hero? Most surely. Judging from his watery, puffy eyes he was also a lover of strong wine. *But he is no silly follower of Bacchus*, Abiel thought bitterly. With the imperial carriage and arrogant tilt of his head, he was the iron oppression of Rome personified.

Once aboard, the two Romans paused to run a critical eye over the decks and towering mast. Abiel walked slowly to them as if they were of no particular interest, satisfied to see he was taller than the centurion, probably stronger, and very much younger.

"May we see the 'magister navis'?" the Centurion asked crisply.

"*I* am the shipmaster."

"Oh? Then forgive me that I expected someone of greater age. Captain, my name is Julius Longidaneas. My legion is the Eighth Augustan."

"I am Abiel Ben Heled of Alexandria."

The two nodded formally. As they did so, Abiel could not help but notice the faded battle scar across the centurion's left eyebrow and cheek. On his left forearm was the scar of a deep wound indeed.

"You have a beautiful ship here, Captain," the Roman went on. "And from a beautiful city as well. I passed through Alexandria several years ago. A fascinating place. I envy anyone who lives there."

"I see little of it myself."

"Yes. A disadvantage of your business and mine, I'm afraid. Captain, I am told by the harbor master that you are bound for Rome with a cargo of free-market grain. I assume that you intend to make the best speed possible, since the profit will be yours."

"We will sail from here in several days, yes," said Abiel. "I intend to go as far west as possible before winter."

"Good. Because I am bound for Rome on imperial business."

"You desire passage, then?"

"I have a contingent of prisoners, Captain—fourteen of them—who have appealed to the emperor's tribunal."

At that Abiel knew a tightening of his stomach. "Prisoners?"

"Yes. And I believe your ship will transport us very well."

Abiel's pulse quickened. Never had he transported slaves or prisoners. Never had anyone been in chains aboard his ship. "Sir," he tried to keep the anger from his voice, "I regret that I have as many passengers now as I can conveniently accommodate . . ."

The optio sneered. "According to the harbor master, you have two hundred and fifty-five—passengers and crew together. You could easily handle one hundred more. Why do you object?"

"Perhaps you object to the prisoners?" the centurion smiled. "Really, Captain, I assure you they will be well guarded, and they are not violent criminals. And of course," he lowered his voice as if to spare Abiel embarrassment, "you are familiar with the law that allows me to charter this ship. There is no need for me to remind you of the obvious."

For a few seconds Abiel stared coldly at the Romans: the

centurion's weathered, scarred face and the smooth face of
the optio, anxious to wield power. Yes, Abiel knew the regulations well enough. With or without his permission, the centurion had the authority to charter the *Athelia* for imperial
service. Once aboard, he would also be technically in charge
of the ship, although he would likely not interfere with its
planned itinerary. Suddenly realizing his fists were clenched,
Abiel opened them slowly and turned to Farnaces, the first
mate, who was watching from the rail. "Tell Alexander to
come here, will you?"

A moment later, Alexander the clerk emerged from the forward hatchway. Alexander was a pale young man who wore
his fingernails long to show he was not an ordinary seaman.
Normally arrogant, his imperial air dissolved in the presence
of the Romans.

Abiel introduced them. "The centurion will bring a group of
prisoners aboard," Abiel said tersely. "And I assume there will
be someone to guard them."

"Myself and three soldiers," rumbled Julius.

"Show him the passenger quarters and accommodations."
Abiel's voice tightened with anger. "Our ship will be under
imperial charter."

"And of course," the optio spoke up, "the centurion will
require a private cabin."

Abiel paused a moment as the trace of a wry smile straightened the corners of his mustache. "Sir," he nodded to the
centurion, "I'm afraid there will be a problem with that."

"A problem?"

"You see, we only have two private cabins. One is mine; the
other belongs to our first officer, the sailmaster."

"Then protocol requires I share your cabin. Why is there a
problem?"

"It is because," Abiel said evenly, "I am a Jew, a son of
Abraham. I am bound by the law of Moses which forbids me
to have a Gentile guest in my home."

Julius' eyes narrowed as Alexander went pale.

Abiel's expression did not change. "You see, my cabin is the
only residence I have. It is my home."

"You are *devoutly Jewish*?" the centurion snapped; and his glare of sudden anger bored into Abiel. "Captain, when I was recently in Caesarea I encountered Jews such as you who obey your invisible God above my emperor. Many of them are dead now for their foolishness. Are you of the same belief as they?"

Abiel had no idea of what had happened in Caesarea, or how many Jews this centurion might have killed. He only knew the countless times he had prayed along with his rabbi in synagogue:

O Master of the Universe, Thou hast commanded us to obey
    Thee.
To meditate on Thy laws day and night.
But the world does not know them.
For the world is Cain and Amalek and Egypt.
The world is Rome—Oh, that their very memory could be
    erased.
But we of Israel were created for this: to obey Thee,
The One True God.

Abiel took a deep breath while his placid expression remained unchanged. "Sir, if you were in my homeland, then you know a devout Jew must obey God above all."

The centurion's scar became more pronounced as he paled in anger.

"Sir, will you *permit* this?" the optio hissed.

For a tense moment the group of men stood in silence. Alexander involuntarily backed away several steps. The centurion slowly ran a big hand down across his eyes and jaw; then quite suddenly his face creased in sardonic amusement. "You Jews," he growled. "By the gods you will be the death of me yet." Through tight lips he spat on the deck. "Very well, Jew. It is only by the mercy of my emperor that you are permitted to worship your silly God at all. Since His Excellency has shown you mercy, I will do the same. Your sailmaster's cabin will do very well. It may even serve me better, since your lunacy may be contagious."

Abiel nodded slowly. "That is well."

Beneath his tight smile the Roman was boiling with anger, and something else as well—weakness or fear? Abiel couldn't be sure.

Later that evening, after Alexander had shown them the passengers' area where the prisoners would be kept, the two soldiers made their way through the streets of Myra back to their quarters at the Tres Tabernae Inn. They strode rapidly through the forest of booths and tarps and haggling traders, but were forced to pause once for a caravan of donkeys laden with mountainous bales of shorn wool. Like some Jews, the donkeys did not know they were supposed to defer to Roman authority. As they waited, the centurion studied the hard face of his assistant. "Something is bothering you. Speak your mind, Gaius; that's an order."

The young soldier's lips curled in disgust. "Sir, was it necessary to allow that Jew to insult you?"

"It was expedient," the centurion said. "A tactical retreat may be the proper action sometimes—but very hard on the spirit."

"Then I take it, sir, that what happened to you in Caesarea did not completely destroy your spirit?"

The centurion eyed his optio curiously. "I don't know, Gaius. But I think perhaps it did."

The young man was startled to hear that. *Yes*, thought Julius. *Well, let him keep his illusions of invincibility. As for me . . . I will anticipate the cool wine at the Tres Tabernae.*

The next day Abiel supervised the loading of three thousand amphorae—tall gracefully shaped wine jars which would remain in the hold until after Abiel sold his cargo of grain in the spring. On the return trip to Alexandria, he planned to stop at the offshore islands of Asia to fill his jars with the good, inexpensive wine of the vineyards there. Of course, the wine would not be inexpensive when he arrived in Alexandria with it. A good profit, then another load of grain for Rome—it was a cycle he had repeated for several years, and it had served him well. With a fast turnaround in Rome's port of Puteoli, he sometimes made two grain runs, or he might handle other cargoes. Ceramics from Arretium and the black wool of Laodicea were always good investments. Pickled fish always sold well in Spain and Italy, and if the price was right, he handled smoked beef or timber. There was always, of course, the constant demand to transport slaves, but Abiel would not touch such a cargo regardless of the profit.

For Abiel, as for all commercial shipmen on the Great Sea, the cycle of trading was interrupted by winter, when all prudent sailors sought a safe port and remained there until spring. Winter brought the cold and darkness, with low clouds and fog to hide the sun, stars, and headlands from the helmsman's eye. There were the howling Etesian winds. Worst of all was the "euraquilo," the sudden vicious storm that could strike and founder a ship without warning. Little wonder, then, that the Great Sea was practically deserted in winter, and Roman regulations regarding government cargo specified, "From the kalends (beginning) of November until the kalends of April, navigation shall be suspended."

Thus was Abiel anxious to leave Myra and sail west again during the few remaining weeks of safe weather. In stentorian tones, he hurried his crew as they stacked the jars in strapped bundles on the lower deck, buffering them with sacks of grain.

In the midst of this hurry, a voice boomed from the dock below: "Abiel Ben Heled!" The shipmaster groaned as he recognized the voice. He crossed the planks to peer down at the dock below. And there, in a sedan chair borne by four muscular slaves, lounged the portly figure of slave dealer Lydas Phlegon, bedecked in his usual scarlet robe and jeweled turban. Seated beside him, with her light-blonde hair twined in a garland, was the most beautiful woman Abiel had ever seen.

"Ah, Ben Heled," Lydas roared. "The gods have smiled that you have stopped in our humble corner of the world."

Abiel reluctantly took his eyes from the woman. "Good afternoon, Lydas. Well, haven't the Romans hung your fat carcass yet, or can't they construct a stout enough cross?"

The bearers in front grinned widely. Abiel's expression did not betray them.

"Ben Heled!" said Lydas. "Do you address an honest businessman thus, who only wishes to take passage on your waxed piece of driftwood?"

"You know I will not haul slaves, Lydas."

"No, no, my dear boy, not on this trip. I only desire passage for myself and," he nodded toward the woman, "for Demaris here. We are traveling together; surely you would not refuse us passage."

The woman looked up then, and her exquisitely slanted blue eyes met Abiel's. Their gaze locked and held; the shipmaster drew in his breath. Never had he felt such a sensation at the mere look of a woman.

She could be Jewish—judging from her sandy hair and blue eyes, a Galilean. But of this he could not be certain. Her full lips, slightly upturned at the corners, revealed a basic good humor, but her haunting eyes spoke of something else—betrayal, and a spirit badly crushed. As Abiel once more took his eyes reluctantly away, he wondered if she were Phlegon's companion. More likely, she was a slave he was delivering to a wealthy client in Rome—the kind who considered it beneath his status to buy slaves from the common markets but instead ordered from traders like Phlegon, who served his selected clientele with discriminating taste. How well she would fit in a patrician setting—and how nice, thought Abiel, it would be to have her aboard . . .

"Very well, Lydas," he said at length. "Perhaps none of my other passengers will know who you are. You may come aboard. If all goes well, we will sail tomorrow evening on the offshore breeze."

"Good!" The buffoonery vanished from Phlegon's face. "You may be insulted by my presence, Ben Heled, but you of course will find my passage money quite acceptable."

"Of course," returned Abiel.

"Then we will be here tomorrow with our baggage."

Abiel sighed as the sedan chair glided swiftly away on the shoulders of the professional bearers. How completely were the tentacles of the sordid world grasping him, he thought. The precious illusion of freedom he had had but a few days ago was dying. Yet a vague warm excitement flickered at the thought of having that lovely woman aboard his ship. *How she reminds me of Ruth* he thought. Not so much in physical appearance, but in the underlying buoyancy her face revealed. But then, in a way, it would not be good to have a constant reminder of Ruth so near. No, it might not be good at all.

The next day, the crew members who had been at liberty came filtering back to the ship. Shortly after the noon hour, Calliades came dragging up the gangway. With his conical wide-brimmed hat and sea bag slung across his shoulder, he could have passed for a vagabond come to look at the pretty ship. Calliades had been visiting a lady friend he had not seen for a long time. It mattered not to him that she was also the lady friend of a hundred other sailors and lived in a house with other friendly ladies. Passing Abiel on the deck he was obviously embarrassed and, to cover it, murmured, "You should have come with me."

"And have a prostitute possess my soul?"

"It would do you good."

"Not when Solomon wrote that her house is the doorway to hell. And for my sake," Abiel grinned slightly, "I hope you didn't tell her you're first officer of the *Athelia*."

"I didn't, Skipper." The sailmaster went on his way to his cabin a little less jauntily. Unlike most pagans, Calliades wasn't proud of his sin. He had been around Abiel enough for that at least.

A short while later, as most of the passengers and crew watched from the rail, the Roman prisoners arrived. In the distance the group of them filed down the wooden steps to the docks. Abiel counted fourteen humans with chains running through manacles on their wrists and necks, linking one prisoner to the other.

"Looks like they all escape or none," commented Farnaces wryly as he watched with Abiel.

The contingent was guarded by three soldiers while the centurion strode ahead. Except for the chains, the prisoners could have been ordinary businessmen, a bit weathered by their travels.

As he watched, Abiel found himself noticing one prisoner in particular: an old man dressed in Roman style with a striped red coat. Accompanied by an unchained friend, a Greek of noble bearing, the prisoner walked energetically despite his age. His face, underlined by a short white beard, was intriguing indeed. It was not the face of a convict; rather, it revealed a gravity of knowledge and gentle cheer together, as if the man was privy to some wonderful secret. Abiel couldn't help but smile. "Look at the third one from the end," he muttered to Farnaces. "The old man."

"Hum. I wonder what *his* crime was."

"I'd wager he's a professional shyster," said Abiel. "With a face like his, he could charm away the contents of anyone's purse." Abiel smiled again and decided he liked the old man, if for no other reason than he was obviously Jewish.

When the prisoners filed up the gangplank, though, Abiel's smile faded. The stark sound of rattling chains violated the freedom he prized aboard his ship. "Where is Alexander?" he barked suddenly to the startled Farnaces. "Tell him to get these people situated and get his papers to my cabin fast. We'll get out of this pesthole."

A short while later a rushed and subdued Alexander arrived at the shipmaster's cabin, wondering what was so irritating the skipper. Grimly Abiel scanned the passenger list and noted that Phlegon had boarded with his woman companion Demaris. Two hundred seventy-six people were now aboard the ship—a fair number. Quickly Abiel looked over the list of valuables some passengers had committed to the ship's strongbox, which was located in the bulkhead of his cabin. At the entry under Lydas Phlegon's name, Abiel drew in his breath. In one leather pouch, three thousand denarii, and five gold bars valued at fifteen thousand denarii commercial standard—a literal fortune. The captain raised his eyes, questioning.

"Now do you see why I am so concerned about having felons aboard?" Alexander said peevishly. "When we are far enough from land, the centurion even intends to let them walk about. At least he will leave their chains on them."

Abiel could not resist a joke. "Where is your confidence, Alexander? The mighty centurion will protect us."

Alexander frowned. "Whom you have insulted beyond reason."

"So I have. So I have. Seriously, Alexander, be sure no one knows of the money Phlegon has in here. Do you understand?"

"Of course!"

Abiel signed the documents and the cargo manifest, and Alexander hastily departed to leave copies on file with the harbor master.

In late afternoon they hauled out of the slip. Shaking the brail lines loose, the crew let the mainsail cascade down from the yardarm. Slowly it filled and billowed in the evening breeze, a great cloud orange-tinted in the evening sun. Slowly the *Athelia* began to glide away, leaving the docks and a few spectators in her gurgling wake.

In deepening twilight, they cleared the harbor, and *Athelia* began to rise and fall in a smooth swell. On the aft deck, Abiel and Calliades stood for a moment in silent concentration until they were sure the three thousand wine jars had not overbalanced them. Then Abiel took the rudder bars so his sailmaster could get some rest before taking charge again during the second watch of night, and the shipmaster was soon alone on the high deck, silhouetted against the evening sky. When they were clear of the bay, Abiel called down orders to Farnaces to stand by to trim sails. Sure of sufficient speed for the maneuver, Abiel confidently swung his ship to seaward, bringing the wind to a point aft of the port beam. At Farnaces' command, his chanting watchmates pivoted the great yardarm, swinging the mainsail. To the alarm of the more nervous passengers, the ship heeled slightly to the wind.

Standing between the rudder bars, gripping them as one would grip the banisters of a narrow stairwell, Abiel steered his ship. He coordinated the two great rudders by treating the bars as if they were reins, attached to the ship's bow as to a horse's bridle. Thus a turn to starboard simply meant pulling back on the right hand bar and pushing forward on the left. Of course, it was not that simple in practice. Because of the ship's configuration, Abiel had to constantly fight a strong tendency to swing windward. At the same time, she was riding the swells diagonally, so he also had to compensate for stern drag, wallow, lead time, and momentum. A sloppy helmsman could give the crew and passengers alike a hard time. But Abiel, observing the evening star, kept her steady and was scarcely aware himself of the concentration required of him.

It was then that his eyes found Demaris among the passengers milling about the lower deck in the cool evening. Clad in a long white woolen tunic, a "stola," she stood alone at the port rail, watching the sea. Abiel knew a vague pleasure that Phlegon was not with her. Apparently she preferred to keep her distance from the slave dealer. She turned from the rail then, gracefully and slowly as she always seemed to move, and looked up toward the aft deck. Again her eyes met Abiel's, and in the dim light Abiel thought he saw her smile. Then with irresistible force, he was swept into the memory of that day years ago in Alexandria when he had first seen Ruth. From the roof of his father's house he had spied her on the street below, carrying a water jar on her hip, and their eyes had met . . .

"O Master of the Universe," Abiel breathed. "Why must this woman have come aboard?"

How long ago now seemed those golden days just before they had landed at Myra. Then, suspended in another world of sun and silence, he had been free and content. *But now,* he thought, *I have Roman soldiers with me, and Roman prisoners, and a slave dealer, and a woman who brings up Ruth before my eyes every time I look at her.* Until they were gone, he knew he would not be free.

CHAPTER 3

*T*HAT NIGHT AFTER THE SECOND WATCH, Abiel lay in the darkness of his cabin while, on the aft deck directly above him, Calliades steered the ship among the stars of night. In the gentle rise and fall of the ship, Abiel at last slept—and dreamed . . .

"Ruth? Ruth, look and see how God in His wisdom guides us on the sea." In the rooftop garden of Ruth's father, the gabbai Shemuel, a synagogue charity officer, Abiel pointed upward toward the night sky, his arm moving in a steady line. "See? There is Aquila, the Eagle, which follows Pegasus, the horse. There, you see? Now, imagine a line running from Altair, the bright star in Aquila, to Pegasus. That line will point you toward Puteoli and Rome."

Ruth Bas Shemuel, her dark eyes gleaming in the starlight, leaned her head closer to Abiel's arm. "You will have to show me Altair again," she said.

He chuckled. "Very well. First find again the summer triangle. There it is. Deneb, Vega, then Altair . . ."

As they drew closer together in the warm evening, her hair brushed his arm, and the fragrance of the cinnamon sachet around her neck teased his senses. He shivered, yet felt strangely warm, and with joyous energy utterly surprised them both by putting his long, bronzed arms around her and drawing her to him.

"Abiel!" she gasped.

He kissed her, smothering any further protests; and in a

moment of delight he felt her resistance melt as she relaxed against him. Then she began to push away.

"Abiel, please! Father may come up here and see us!"

They stood staring at one another wordlessly. In the starlight Abiel could see her eyes were narrowed as she breathed through parted lips, and he knew he had awakened in her the same desire as in himself, the wonderful desire God had given to men and women. "Oh Ruth," he breathed. "Ruth. If I were to ask my father to arrange with yours for our betrothal . . . would you be willing?"

"Oh, Abiel. *Ohavie*—my love. How long I've waited for you to say it! Ask my father for me. Of course I am willing!"

"And you will have my sons?"

She nodded wordlessly. They stared at one another awkwardly for a moment. Suddenly she gave that mischievous grin that so delighted him. "And how do you know they will be sons?"

"Of course they will be sons!" Abiel Ben Heled threw back his head and laughed in the late summer evening. "Else how would they be shipmen?" He reached for her again—and awoke in the solitary darkness of his cabin, his arms outstretched to nothing.

With a deep sigh the shipmaster looked up from his pallet. "O Master of the Universe," he prayed softly, "why do you torment me with dreams of her when she can never be mine? For you know she is dead to me, and I am dead to her." Deep in the darkness he cast his eyes upward. He knew why he had dreamed of her. Yes. He should not let his mind wander so when gazing at the woman Demaris.

Through the open shutters of his window, the brilliant liquid stars shone just as they had on that night three years ago in Alexandria, but tonight his topsails formed a dark outline against them. Abiel watched as the sails swept slowly across the Twins of the Sky, Castor and Pollux. The cluster of stars was devoured by the sails, only to be spewed out in shining pieces on the return swing.

"Gemini to starboard," Abiel muttered. From that reckoning alone he knew several things: that the last watch of night had begun, that the ship was tacking on a southwesterly course, which in turn meant the headwind had not changed since he'd left the helm. Abiel made a mental note of the wind and the moderate swell and saw in them no danger. In mid-autumn, even lonely and saddened shipmasters must be wary of the signs of wind and sea. But tonight he saw in them no danger.

Outside in the darkness, Calliades called out muted orders. In response came the thumping of the sailors' bare feet on the run. Abiel felt the ship begin a gradual turn to starboard, watched the stars wheel slowly around, and heard the night watch call cadence as they hauled the great yardarm around. With that, the ship rolled toward her starboard rail, now on a new tack.

Abiel lay still, feeling the ship. She was picking up speed. But now, as she dipped down each swell, Abiel could sense a dull thud from far forward at the bow, and a barely detectable shudder. Annoyed, he rose up on one elbow, wondering if Calliades could feel it, too. The bow was driving down too far, as it often did on a port tack, and Abiel would probably have to get out of bed to get his ship on trim. But then the halyard winch rumbled overhead as Calliades lowered the yardarm down the mast a bit, in effect lowering the ship's center of effort. Soon the tremor ceased as *Athelia* planed smoothly into the swells.

Very good. Very good. Abiel lay back down again. Probably none of the crew knew that "the rabbi" was lying awake, monitoring their performance. But did he not have a right to be demanding and jealous of the way others treated what was now his only love? He grimaced at that thought and, on impulse, rose from the pallet and called out the window to the deck above. "Calliades, have someone bring a light in here, will you?" Then he crawled back under the woolen covers. "A curse on this darkness."

The cabin door opened and old Coos entered, carrying a small bronze lamp which he ceremoniously matched to the swinging of the captain's lamp, a beautifully burnished copper lantern which had once been the stern marker of a small ship.

"Thank you," Abiel said brusquely as the cabin brightened.

"A beautiful night it is out there, sir," said Coos. In the yellow light the old man grinned widely, revealing his broken and missing teeth, eloquent testimony to many a youthful brawl in dockside taverns. Coos, too, was a man who had no wife or sons to follow him—not officially anyway. Yet his advancing age and childlessness seemed not to dampen his cheerful outlook at all.

So why for us Jews, Abiel wondered, *must everything have eternal significance?*

"I will bring you some water for your basin, sir," said Coos.

"Thank you."

Soon the old seaman was back with a pitcher of fresh water drawn from the bow tank. The *Athelia* had two such tanks made of planks and waterproofed fabric. One tank contained ten thousand gallons of fresh water; the other held live fish for the crew and first-class passengers. Coos placed the pitcher in a box on the washstand; then, sensing the captain was not in a mood for talking, smiled and left.

Abiel lay a few minutes watching the lamp leave a circular plume of smoke as it swung back and forth, yet the light gave him little of the comfort he desired. After his dream of Ruth, there were simply too many ghosts in the rising and falling shadows. Sighing, he got up, slipped on his wool tunic, took a mouthful of wine, and went out into the night. There was no problem in finding the steps. With the ease of a cat he climbed them to the aft deck where Calliades of Rhodes manned the helm.

Standing between the rudder bars, Calliades acknowledged the captain's dim approach with a curt nod, as Abiel walked past him to spit the wine over the rail. "So, the magister cannot sleep again?"

"Not when I have dreamed of Ruth again," Abiel murmured. "Curse the memory of her."

Calliades shrugged. "So . . . in place of her you have this."

Around them in the clear autumn night hung the stars— myriads of them, breathtaking, thousands upon thousands shimmering with a wet luster. In the crystal air the Milky Way spread overhead like glowing dust against the velvet black. Abiel watched the sky a few minutes. "You know," he turned to Calliades, "they remind me of that celebration in the harbor when I was a boy."

"What celebration?"

"In the harbor at Alexandria one night there was a pageant to celebrate how Augustus was supposed to have rid the sea of pirates. There must have been hundreds of catapults on triremes in the harbor. When the music reached a crescendo, they sent the Greek fire* arching across the sky. That was quite a spectacle."

"I imagine so."

"Even that cannot compare with this, though." Abiel tried to remember the words Isaiah the prophet had written of nights like this: "Lift up your eyes on high and see who has created these stars, the One who leads forth their host by number, He calls them all by name; because of the greatness of his might and the strength of His power not one of them is missing."

Abiel liked to think that, in leading forth the stars, God also led men like himself across the sea. Each night the celestial pathfinders came forth: Perseus rushed to rescue the chained Andromeda. Hercules bent to his labors, and Orion fled the fatal scorpion. As the immortal characters passed overhead each night in their eternal journey from east to west, seamen learned to locate among them such lines of direction as the one from Jaffa to the Pillars of Hercules. Meanwhile the center star in the Northern Dragon hung steadily in the same place to show the helmsman true north.† With directional references thus fixed, seamen could navigate by dead reckoning, estimating their wind drift and speed.

On this night, *Athelia* sailed not only by the stars, but through them; they reflected in the swells beneath them and shimmered above and ahead. As the bow rose skyward with each swell, they beckoned the ship on to an unknown destiny.

---

*Balls of pitch mixed with naptha—first-century napalm.
†Due to precession, the slow wobbling of the Earth on its axis, the North Star for first-century navigators was not Polaris but Thuban, middle star in the constellation Draco.

The night went on. Slowly the eastern sky lost its sheen of black and, except for Venus in lonely splendor, the stars melted into a grayish blue of dawn. The swells emerged as newly created, reflecting on their cold glassy sides the glowing sky, and the main deck of the *Athelia* emerged from night wet with dew. Scattered over the deck were blanket rolls, sleeping bags, and small tents of those passengers who preferred to sleep in the open rather than in the lower passenger hold. They sprawled half out of their shelters like bodies scattered in the wake of a fierce battle. With the light of dawn, though, the corpses began coming to life, and a few ghostly figures staggered toward the passageway leading to the latrine in the aft deck overhang. The air was cool and fresh with a touch of salt, and smoke from the galley carried the heady aroma of baking bread and fish.

As usual, Abiel paid a morning inspection visit to the galley which lay on the deck just below and forward of his cabin. The "kitchen" ran the width of the ship and was enclosed fore and aft by bulkheads containing lockers for the pots and pans. Against the forward bulkhead was the firepit. Abiel always inspected it carefully to be sure the bed of sand was deep enough beneath the clay-encased grating and the tiles and smoke hole free of cooking grease. The cook knew very well that failing to keep them that way would mean his dismissal.

As Abiel made his inspections, Alexander arrived to tally the meals for the first-class passengers who had not brought along their own food, but ate the ship's fare. He and Abiel exchanged curt greetings.

For lunch, the cook announced proudly, there would be *corba*, a soup made of tomatoes, fish, and peppers.

"It sounds good," Abiel said, as he paused to sample a piece of the warm, fragrant bread. Strange to think how one can look forward to such simple pleasures. The captain pronounced the bread good, his deep voice resonant in the galley confines. "Ah, and why did the Creator bless me with such superior cooks? You are all worth a king's ransom."

The cook beamed with pleasure. His helper, Plautus, a

simple-minded former slave, grinned as his head bobbed, fawning in appreciation. Alexander watched the display with unfeigned disgust. Quite deliberately his high voice interrupted them. "Oh, Captain . . ."

"What is it, Alexander?"

"I must inform you that the merchant, Lydas Phlegon, wishes to see you on a private matter."

"Has he a complaint?"

"No. It is a matter of private business. Given his status, I assume you will see him quickly?"

"Perhaps sometime."

"I told him you would see him after breakfast this morning in your cabin." Alexander paused to enjoy the irritation on his captain's face. "He says the business is urgent. Who knows? Perhaps he wants to buy Plautus."

Immediate fear shot across Plautus' vacuous face, and it took Abiel and the cook several minutes to assure him he was no longer a slave and could not be purchased by anyone. The captain then turned coldly to Alexander. "A word to the wise. Good clerks may be hard to find, but not *that* hard." Leaving the galley, he muttered angrily, "Too bad that Alexander is not a clerk for Phlegon. The two would get along beautifully."

Shortly after breakfast Abiel found himself seated in his cabin across the table from the slave merchant. At Phlegon's insistence he closed the shutters so only the slowly swinging lamp illuminated the merchant's soft, puffy face. Beneath his turban, Phlegon's eyes appeared half closed.

"What is your business, Lydas?" Abiel growled. "I must soon take the helm, so be brief."

Lydas raised his eyes in mock surprise. "Is there no wine to grace a meeting of business associates?"

"No," said Abiel.

Lydas sighed. "Very well, Ben Heled. As you know I make it my business to keep up with the affairs of shipmen. The world of commerce, you know. Now, am I correct that you did not spend this past winter in Alexandria?"

"No, I did not."

"Nor the year before!" said Phlegon quickly. "My, my! For

two years you neglect your relatives and friends. That is most *un*-Jewish of you, Abiel."

"I thought this concerned business."

"This *is* business, my dear boy. Listen. It has surely occurred to you that if you did not stop at some port this winter, but sailed directly on to Rome, then you could unload your grain this winter and be back on schedule to spend next winter in Alexandria with your family and friends."

Abiel was unsure of what to make of this. He had no desire, of course, to tell Phlegon he had not *wanted* to be in Alexandria. He had not wanted to be anywhere near Ruth Bas Shemuel. "Lydas, I am touched by your concern," he said, "if surprised."

Phlegon smiled. "Well, Abiel, you see I also have a reason of my own that I must be in Rome this winter. It, uh, concerns that considerable sum of money I have in your strongbox. It is most important that I deliver that money to Rome this winter, by the Feast of Saturnalia."

"Lydas . . ." Abiel shook his head with an exasperated smile. "When you came aboard my ship, you knew very well we would not reach Rome by winter! With this headwind, which isn't likely to change, we will be lucky to reach Cnidus. And you know very well the dangers of sailing much later than the Fast of the Day of Atonement."

"That is true," Lydas said quickly. "But I hope you realize, Abiel, I would not ask this of most shipmasters. But I know your skill, and the skill of your sailmaster. You could both judge the weather and conserve your chances; and I believe we could make it with little danger."

Abiel shook his head. "I am flattered by your confidence. But I have two hundred and seventy-four other people aboard this ship. I will not risk their safety for the sake of your business—which I detest at any rate."

The merchant's flaccid face remained expressionless, although his voice rose slightly. "Ben Heled, you do not realize how vitally important it is to me that I be in Rome this winter. So consider my offer. I am prepared to pay you a substantial sum, a bonus shall we say, if you will sail on . . ."

"Phlegon," Abiel waved his hand wearily. "Do you think I would risk my passengers and ship for any amount you could give me?"

"Ben Heled, there is nothing in your precious Jewish law to prevent you doing this! You could take the money and give it to the temple of your God! He would bless you!"

"I'm sorry. It is out of the question."

The merchant's face grew cold. "I was hoping to find you more reasonable."

"I am being *very* reasonable. We both know of too many ships on the bottom of the sea now who tempted fate in the winter. And besides," Abiel's mustache twitched upward in a grin, "*I* am not in command of this ship anyway, if you will remember. If you wish to bribe someone, see the centurion."

"He is in command of this ship in name only," spat Phlegon. "I will not bother myself beseeching him."

Abiel's grin widened. It was general knowledge among shipmen that Lydas Phlegon dealt not only in slaves, but in stolen merchandise. He would not go to the centurion, who might ask embarrassing questions.

"I must be about my work, Lydas," Abiel yawned and stretched.

The merchant, plainly angry, rose to his feet. "Ben Heled," he hissed, "what will be the reward of your vaunted virtue? Nothing, I dare say. You are a fool to refuse my offer. A fool!"

"That may well be," said Abiel. Then, on sudden impulse, he stopped Phlegon. "Before you go, Lydas, one question. Who is the woman traveling with you?"

"She is a recent purchase who I am taking to a client in Ravenna, if it is any of your concern. But she is only incidental to this trip. Obviously, I could make no profit transporting only one slave."

"Obviously."

Phlegon's eyes narrowed. "And what is your interest in her, Ben Heled?"

"Oh, nothing really." Abiel waved his hand too casually. "I only wondered if she was your wife. Who knows? Perhaps you had succumbed to the lure of marriage."

"Marriage! Hardly necessary." The merchant snorted and slammed the cabin door as he left.

Abiel sat for a moment, musing. He had to admit to a feeling of relief. It was tragic enough that the beautiful Demaris should be a slave. How much more tragic if she were Phlegon's wife.

CHAPTER 4

*A*LL THAT MORNING Abiel fought the headwind that blew steadily from the northwest. The topside crew had an easy time of it, because they only had to adjust the sails when he changed tacks. Otherwise, all they could do was tug the yardarm as far fore and aft as it would go; it was up to the helmsman to steer the closest heading to northwest that the wind would allow. This Abiel did by every so often pointing the ship windward until the sail began to ripple and luff, then steering a little in the opposite direction until it billowed full again. This would be the heading at which the sail developed its best power, and would be as close to northwest as he could steer. He would hold that heading until the wind changed again. Meanwhile, throughout the day, Farnaces, the first mate, rotated the bronze azimuth ring to compensate for the sun's movement across the sky.

Such steering was hard work, especially on a ship like *Athelia*, which had a strong tendency to "weathervane" into the wind. Her designer and builder, M. Lattius of Alexandria, had built four ships with the same hull design. In talking with the master of one of them, the *Taurus Ruber*, Abiel had found that he had the same problem. It could be remedied easily, of course, if one were willing to sacrifice some speed. Farnaces, watching his captain lean into the rudder bars, suggested it. "Shall we brail up the sail aft of the mast, sir?"

"No," called Abiel. "Leave 'em all full. I want to make some distance today!"

Thus when midday came, Abiel was near exhaustion and happy to be relieved by Farnaces. In his cabin, he welcomed the chance to rest a few moments and savor the pungent soup his cook had prepared. The relaxation, though, did not last. He had no sooner finished the meal than he was startled by sudden shouting out on deck—angry cries mixed with the grunts and snarls of fighting men. A heavy object thudded against the side of his cabin.

"What on earth?" Abiel jerked the cabin door open to see, in the bright sunlight, the three Roman soldiers and five of his crewmen punching and cursing. Big Jabo's head snapped back with a blow and he fell to the deck almost at Abiel's feet, only to roll and kick the feet from under a Roman, who fell heavily on his back. In an instant Jabo was on top of him, pounding the soldier across the head with his own helmet. Horrified, Abiel grabbed the helmet from his crewman's upraised hand. "Enough! Stop this!" he roared. "Stop the fighting!"

At the remarkable power of his voice, the fighters paused uncertainly; then heard the centurion coming at a run. "Attention! Legionnaires, attention!"

The two soldiers who were still able to stand immediately snapped to attention, throwing their right hands across their chests in a closed-fisted salute. As they did so, Plautus punched the bigger one in the mouth. Abiel lunged, pinning his crewman in a bearhug, and spun him away from the Roman.

"They were going to throw you overboard!" Plautus blubbered, his eyes wide in terror and rage. "They were going to throw you overboard!"

"No one will throw me overboard, Plautus! Quiet down! Be quiet now."

And then the deck was quiet except for a moan from the bloodied soldier lying on the planks and murmurs from a gathering crowd of appalled passengers.

The physician Lucanus knelt to wipe blood from the soldier's face and gingerly examine an ugly welt on his forehead. The fallen Roman sat up suddenly and brushed him aside. "I'm all right, Greek! If I need your attention I'll tell you!"

"Let him examine your cut," said the centurion curtly. Then to Abiel, "What happened here, Captain?"

"I don't know . . . yet." Abiel's eyes slowly swept the gathered men. "But you may be sure I will find out."

The seamen began talking at once. At this Julius held up his hand. "Silence!" He turned to Abiel. "No, Captain, *you* may be sure *I* will find out! I'm sure you know the seriousness of assaulting a Roman!" The centurion walked slowly over to Abiel and eyed him coldly, their faces only several inches apart. "Three days ago I let it pass when you insulted both the emperor and me with your barbaric beliefs. But this . . . *this* will not pass! Your men who assaulted mine will answer before a Roman court."

Abiel felt a cold anger rising and knew he must control it. *His* men, on *his* ship? Hades would release the dead first. "I assume then *your* men will be punished as well if they assaulted mine?"

"Nonsense! If my men had been at all serious, your men would be dead now."

"And if my seamen had used their knives, so would yours."

That statement was pure bluff, of course. Seamen carried their knives for splicing line, or cutting it in emergencies, but it was an unwritten law that they would never use the knives as weapons. In the wildest tavern brawl, Abiel had never yet seen a seaman use his knife. Still, his words caused the centurion to pause, and Abiel seized his initiative. "Isn't it lawful we investigate what happened before anyone is charged?"

On this bright afternoon Julius' head was yet tender from too much wine the night before. Now, in the face of this undaunted Jew, it positively ached. "I *told* you, Captain, I would find out what happened. Lacking the gift of sorcery, that means I must conduct an investigation, doesn't it?" Slowly he turned away from Abiel to Lucanus. "Physician, I want a description on parchment of any wounds my men suffered in this. And, men, we will question each one of you individually in the captain's cabin, beginning in a few minutes. I trust the Jew's God will allow me into the cabin on business."

Coarse laughter echoed from Gaius and the other soldiers.

"Meanwhile," the centurion went on, "none of you are to discuss this incident among yourselves. Gaius, make sure these seamen keep their mouths shut. And see that no one leaves the group. We will have no one fabricating their tales together. And, Captain, summon your clerk to take depositions."

At the centurion's crisp commands, the seamen began to grow nervous, realizing quite suddenly they could be in a great deal of trouble.

"Relax, men," Abiel murmured as he passed them. "All will be well."

They all wore mournful looks—Naso, Marius, Munatus, and Plautus, plus a sailor called simply "Troas" after the city he had come from. Abiel could remember the time and place he had hired each one. They were unshaven, generally unwashed, and broken-toothed. But they were good, dependable, and unquestioning men. Being children of the sea, they did not plan their tomorrows. They demanded little and expected little, and Abiel determined in his heart that nothing would befall them.

As they situated the chairs at his cabin table, Abiel's mind raced, and by the time they took their seats he had arrived at a hopeful strategy. The centurion removed his helmet, and Abiel noted with pleasure the streaks of gray in his short curly hair. *It seems even the gods grow old.* Judging from the centurion's puffy eyes, he likely felt very old this morning as well, and Abiel guessed correctly he would like to have this over as quickly as possible. So the shipmaster spoke up quickly. "Sir, with your permission, I'd like to call Seaman Plautus as our first witness."

"For any particular reason?"

"Simply that he is the most truthful man I have ever known. I believe hearing him first will help shorten this hearing."

Not surprisingly, Julius agreed. So, as Alexander took written record, the first witness to enter was the cook's helper, Plautus, still upset and obviously distraught.

"Here," Abiel said gently, motioning him toward the table.

Julius, eyeing their witness with some disgust, noticed the triangular scar in his earlobe. "Is this man a slave?"

"I do not keep slaves," said Abiel. "Plautus' former owner dismissed him. I have his manumission papers in my strongbox. I hired him as a freedman on Corsica." Abiel didn't bother telling the centurion just why he had hired Plautus— that the man had been starving, with no money and no place to go. What would a Roman know of pity?

Plautus looked suddenly at both of them, his eyes open wide in alarm. "They were going to throw the captain . . . Abiel . . . overboard!" he slurred.

"If not a slave, is this man an idiot?" asked Julius sharply.

"Not an idiot," said Abiel. "He is only slow of thought and speech, and has a child's mind. That is why I told you he is the most honest man I know." Turning to Plautus, he questioned gently. "*Who* was going to throw me overboard, Plautus?"

"The soldiers!" said Plautus.

"How do you know?"

"They *said* they were! I heard them say . . . say they were."

"What sort of absurdity . . . ?" Julius growled, growing angry. "Come now! Which soldiers said such a thing? When?"

Plautus blinked and swallowed. "The big soldier," he said stubbornly, holding his hands wide apart. "The big one with the blue sleeves. I heard him! One soldier said they would make the captain live in the latrine. Then the big one laughed and said no—they would throw him overboard instead." Plautus' lip began trembling. "And so I hit him with my . . . hand . . . and they threw me down. Then I hit him again. Then Jabo and Troas came to help me . . ."

"And then," Abiel smiled at the centurion, "the brawl began."

The centurion's lips pursed in thought. He drummed his fingers on the table, then flicked a bit of dust from his helmet. On his face was a hint of disappointment. "Very well," he growled, "let us hear what the 'big soldier' has to say."

So the next witness was the optio, Gaius. He was tall enough that the light from the hanging lamp gleamed in his face, and his swollen lip and eye resembled the tragic mask from a Greek drama. Saluting smartly, he held it until re-turned by the centurion.

"Gaius," Julius said wearily, "can you tell us really how this fight started? What actually happened?"

"There is little to tell, sir," said Gaius, his deep voice rum-bling in the cabin. "We had just finished our noon chow. We were going back to bring the prisoners for theirs . . . just joking and talking out there. Then all of a sudden that idiot just comes out of nowhere. He began hitting and clawing me, and screaming."

"Seaman Plautus?"

"The sailor who was in here first, yes sir. Then a few more of this Jew's crew joined him. Next thing I knew, we were in the middle of a pretty good fight. You should have let us wipe the deck with them, sir."

The centurion's mouth hardened into a straight line. "Very well, now. Before the fight, you said you were joking. What were you joking about?"

"Sir, we were just joking. That's all."

"What about? What were you saying among yourselves?"

Gaius was obviously embarrassed. Then his face hardened. "Sir, all respect to you, sir. But we were talking about how this Jew . . ." he cocked his head toward Abiel, "has insulted you in front of everyone aboard this ship. He thinks he is too good to share his cabin with a Gentile dog. All respects, sir, but that is what this Jew thinks you are. And so . . . we were only laughing about, if we threw him out of his cabin and made him live in the latrine, then you could take his cabin since it wouldn't be his home anymore. That is all we were doing, sir. Jesting."

"What was said about throwing the captain overboard?"

"Just . . ." Gaius looked coldly at Abiel, "just that the la-trine is too good for him, I said. I said we should throw him overboard instead. I guess that idiot Plautus thought we were really going to do it. He just came out of nowhere."

Abiel turned his head slightly so his mustache and beard hid the grin he could not suppress. "May I ask your optio a question?" he said.

"It would be best if I asked it!" Julius snapped, annoyed that Plautus' testimony had been confirmed.

"Ask him at what point my other seamen joined the fight."

Gaius shrugged. "I suppose when that idiot began his screaming."

"Ask him," said Abiel, "how many times they threw Plautus to the deck."

The answer was three times. "He wouldn't quit," said Gaius. "He kept bouncing back like an inflated bladder."

Abiel turned quietly to the centurion. "So it would seem that settles the question."

"Does it?"

"Was it an assault by my men on your soldiers? Or simply my crewmen coming to the aid of a shipmate, who was defending his captain against threats from your men?"

Julius' face colored. "What he in his dim mind *perceived* to be threats, Captain! And only after you invited such talk by insulting me yesterday!"

Gaius was dismissed then; and when the soldier was gone, Julius scowled at the table top for a few minutes. He would like nothing better than to humble this Jew sitting next to him. Yet there was no question the Jew had won.

"Very well," the centurion said tightly. "This being an unusual situation, here is what I will do. I will take possession of the testimony your clerk has recorded. You will first sign the parchment . . ."

"I will gladly sign," said Abiel.

A tighter edge crept into Julius' voice. "Then, as long as you and your crew treat my men and me with the proper respect, I will not implead charges. Be sure your men understand this."

"Good. And will you instruct your men to do likewise?"

"My men need no such instruction."

Abiel was tempted to argue that point. But, noting the centurion's rising anger, thought it better to be quiet and accept what he had won. "In that case, may we tell the men they are dismissed? Mine need to be about their work."

The centurion signaled with his hand for the parchment, which Abiel read and signed. Alexander was dismissed. Then, still flushed with anger, the centurion rolled up the transcript and took his helmet. At the cabin door, he paused as if on sudden thought, and turned back to Abiel. "Ben Heled, are you really an expert in your Jewish Scriptures?"

"I have studied them from my youth," said Abiel, surprised. "It is my intention to live by them."

"You are obviously serious about it. Tell me, then, is it really in your Scriptures that a Gentile may not share your cabin? Are your Scriptures really so detailed?"

Abiel paused. All of his life he had debated the Scriptures with fellow Jews, often for hours on end. Now, in the presence of this Roman, he felt inexplicably tongue-tied. "Sir, there is no passage of Scripture concerning a ship's cabin as such. Yet the commandment is there."

"You must explain better than that."

Abiel could not believe that he was answering the questions of a Roman about Jewish Scripture. He hardly knew where to begin. "Sir, you see, when my people conquered the pagan tribes of Canaan many generations ago, God warned through Moses that we were to remain forever separate from them. 'Sanctify, or set yourselves apart,' the Lord commanded, 'and be ye holy.' That command has not changed."

Julius, now back at the table, sat down. With head tilted back slightly he eyed Abiel. "A command of separation."

"From those who do not know God," said Abiel evenly. "Our rabbis have interpreted this separation to mean many things, and one is that a devout Jew should not have Gentiles as guests in his home."

The centurion arched his eyebrows sarcastically as an understanding seemed to dawn in his face.

"We take this command most seriously," Abiel went on. "Over thousands of years we Jews have conquered, and we have been conquered. Yet we are still the separate people God commanded us to be. And when you Romans are gone," Abiel smiled tightly, "we will remain . . . separate."

The Roman nodded slowly as if in deep thought; then shook his head and chuckled wryly. "Ben Heled, either my sanity is finally leaving me, or I am beginning to understand you Jews at last. Perhaps . . . perhaps when I was serving in Caesarea, if I had understood men like you, I could have avoided some mistakes."

Abiel looked up steadily. "Mistakes?"

"You must remember, when I first came aboard, I spoke of some Jews like you in Caesarea. They listened to their law instead of my emperor, and they died for their foolishness."

Abiel's voice was utterly cold. "How many Jews?"

"I don't really know." The Roman shrugged slightly. "And it does not matter to me how many there were. I am not 'confessing' a wrongdoing to you, Captain. If anything, let it be a warning."

"You spoke of a mistake."

"A mistake, yes, in that I underestimated the spirit of men like you, because I did not understand what you believe. And I did not understand as well the fact that my own Roman procurator was afraid of you. I did not understand how badly he wanted to appease you, to grovel before you and placate you. Because of that, I was made a sacrifice, Ben Heled." The centurion paused, and hatred flashed from his dark eyes. "You see, Captain, it is not the normal thing for someone with the rank of primipilus to play nursemaid to a group of prisoners! But I was deserted by my own government. My command was taken from me; I was forced to tuck my tail and run like a whipped dog when I had done no wrong. And it was all to placate you Jews."

The centurion gave a harsh laugh—more a snarl—and grated his helmet on the table as Abiel wondered if he were still a bit drunk.

"No one," Julius went on, "no one in the entire empire gets away with what you Jews get away with. You and your bizarre belief in some invisible God you say is greater than the emperor. And our emperor—hah!—he looks the other way and pretends he doesn't hear when you talk of your 'Messiah' who will conquer Rome for you." The centurion threw back his head and laughed harshly. "That is a good question for you, Ben Heled! So you know your Scriptures, do you? Then tell me about your 'Messiah.' I want to know if your beliefs are as insane as the ones they have in Judea."

Throughout the centurion's tirade, Abiel's expression had remained cold, his eyes steely. For a moment the two men stared at one another, neither dropping his gaze. "Where did you hear of the Messiah?" said Abiel.

"In Caesarea. Where else?"

"If I tell you of Him, you will not like what you hear."

A sneer crossed Julius' face. "Have I not been repeatedly insulted by you people? By now I should be used to it! Tell me about your Messiah, Ben Heled."

Abiel's gaze never left the centurion. "I will tell you, but not in my words. Many generations ago, one of our prophets, Isaiah, wrote of the Messiah: 'For a child will be born to us, a son will be given to us, and the government will rest upon His shoulders; and His name will be called Wonderful Counselor, Mighty God, Eternal Father, Prince of Peace. There will be no end to the increase of His government.'

"And our prophet King David wrote that the Messiah will be given the nations of the earth for His inheritance, and the very ends of the earth for His possession. He will rule them all with a rod of iron. *That* is the Messiah. And He is coming."

The air in the cabin was oppressive. "Then, Captain," the centurion said coldly, "you actually expect him to overthrow Rome?"

"Yes. He will rule the world. That includes Rome. And I will tell you more. It is our hope that if enough Jews keep the Scriptures and obey them as I am doing, then God will look upon us with favor, and Messiah will come."

Julius shook his head slowly. "Not in a thousand years, Ben Heled. But if you Jews *really* believe this, it is no wonder you cannot be governed." For a few moments he eyed Abiel contemptuously. "Very well, Captain. You have had your say. Now it is time for mine; and I will tell you something I suspect may rattle your religious arrogance. One of the prisoners traveling with me is a Roman Jew named Paul. He is an old man, Paul the Aged. And *he* has never said such a seditious thing that this Messiah will overthrow Rome."

"By chance, is Paul that small old man in the striped coat?"

"He is. And he has never said your Messiah will conquer the world."

"Then this Paul obviously does not know the Scriptures."

"On the contrary, Captain!" Julius' eyes flashed in triumph. "He was once a rabbi! He is *quite* learned in your Scriptures. He is able to debate them in five languages, I am told. He has traveled the world, and he has made legions of converts to his teachings . . ."

"His teachings?"

"Yes. His teaching that . . ." Julius' voice trailed off as he raised his eyebrows, "your Messiah has already come."

It took a moment for the words to sink in, and Abiel knew a rising constriction in his chest as the centurion's wolfish smile grew wider. "Have you ever heard of such a thing, Ben Heled?" Julius asked.

"I have heard of false messiahs, yes."

"Paul says He is not false."

"He certainly is. By chance, is Paul's so-called Messiah a crucified Nazarene named Jesus?"

"Yes. Why yes! Then you've heard of Him."

"I have had the great misfortune to hear of Him, yes."

"How?"

"It doesn't matter how." Abiel's voice shook slightly. Yes, he had heard of the false Messiah. Through his mind passed the terrible thing which had happened to his Ruth and her father Shemuel—all because of this Nazarene deceiver named Jesus. He wanted to scream in rage. Realizing his knuckles were white, he slowly unclenched his huge fists on the table.

Julius, watching him with satisfaction, chuckled. "You fools," he murmured. "You Jewish fools. You talk about your mighty God and your mighty Messiah—and you can't even agree on who He is. You can't even agree if He has come or not!" The Roman laughed, his anger appeased somewhat now that he had, at last, rattled the composure of this Jew and humbled him. "Perhaps I should tell you, Captain, the reason Paul is an imperial prisoner is that your kinsmen in Judea desired so badly to kill him that he was forced to appeal to Caesar and get out of Judea just to save his life. Now, judging from your reaction to him, I assume you would like to see him dead as well?"

"He deserves death," Abiel breathed. "How richly he deserves it. But you needn't worry that I would harm him. I am a shipmaster . . ."

"Good." With that, the centurion rose from the table, inspected his silvered helmet in the lamplight, and slipped it on. "Ben Heled," he said offhandedly as he inspected the copper work of Abiel's lamp, "if you Jews don't kill me, you may well warp my mind beyond repair. But there is one thing I think I understand about you. You have the deep thoughts of an old man, but you practice them with the recklessness of a youth. That's a dangerous combination, Captain. So be careful. It could bring you much grief."

CHAPTER 5

*I*T WAS NOW well into the afternoon. Abiel took a few moments to collect his thoughts. Then, before relieving Farnaces at the helm, he mingled for a while with the passengers on the main deck, who had been unsettled by the morning's events. For some of them it was frightening enough just being on the water, without having the two ship's commanders at each other's throats as well. So Abiel walked among them, talking of the wind as if the morning's fight was not worth discussing, assuring his passengers that, even though the distant coastline appeared stationary, they really *were* moving west. All the while, his eyes searched for the woman Demaris; he was vaguely disappointed that she was nowhere to be seen.

That done, he took the rudder bars from Farnaces and resumed his fight with the northwest wind. To take his mind off of the morning's turmoil, he watched the passengers below on the main deck, and he suddenly realized he was wishing Demaris would walk about. But she remained below deck, probably reading or perhaps taking a nap as many passengers did in the afternoon. And on second thought, it was best that he not see her.

A few prisoners with their chains draped from their necks walked about, taking their exercise for the day, Abiel supposed. But then he stiffened to see the old man in the striped coat, Paul. The deceiver walked with his friend, Lucanus the physician, and was surrounded as well by a small, animated audience. How was it that Paul, even with felon's chains running from wrists to neck, could attract people to him? Abiel seethed at the falsehood he knew must be poisoning those listeners.

As much as he detested having chained humans aboard his ship, how glad he would be to see Paul chained in the lowest hold. Once a rabbi? It was inconceivable. But now, for some unexplainable reason, he was a traitor to the faith, spreading that ever-growing falsehood of Jesus.

"O Master of the Universe," Abiel murmured aloud. "Please do not bring calamity on my ship because this deceiver Paul is aboard. Oh, in Rome may the Romans do to him what my kinsmen in Judea could not. There may his lying tongue be silenced in the grave at last."

The prayer brought no relief, however, and during all of that afternoon the shadow of the Nazarene haunted Abiel as if he were a fugitive aboard his own ship. He fought the memories washing over him, but irresistibly his mind was drawn back to the day years ago when he had first heard Shemuel speak of Jesus the Nazarene. Oh that that day had never been conceived in the dawn . . .

It had been a dismal morning in February. But a glowing charcoal fire had given delightful heat and window tapestries shut out the rain and cold as Abiel and his future father-in-law studied Torah together. Studying Torah with Shemuel was never dull, for the gabbai delighted in discussing portions of Scripture Abiel had never heard. This day, however, Shemuel seemed pensive and thoughtful, and the passage of Scripture he read—from the Psalms of David—was the strangest that Abiel had ever heard.

"Listen to this, Abiel," Shemuel said as he found his place in the ornate scroll and read, "'I am poured out like water, and all my bones are out of joint; My heart is like wax; it is melted within me. My strength is dried up like a potsherd, and my tongue cleaves to my jaws; and thou dost lay me in the dust of death. For dogs [Gentiles] have surrounded me; a band of evildoers has encompassed me; they pierced my hands and my feet. I can count all my bones. They look, they stare at me; they divide my garments among them, and for my clothing they cast lots.'"

Slowly Shemuel looked up from the scroll, his face troubled. "My son, what do you suppose King David was describing in this passage?"

Abiel shook his head. "I cannot tell."

"Nor can I," said Shemuel. "But I have an idea of what it may be. Think again of what I have just read. Hands and feet pierced . . . dislocated bones so that he can count every one of them . . . thirst, nakedness. What has David described? It is something the Romans have done to Jews by the thousands."

Abiel thought a moment. "Why . . . the feelings of someone who has been crucified!"

"Precisely. But David wrote this over a thousand years ago, Abiel, when crucifixion was unknown in Israel. My question is . . . *why* did he write this?"

Abiel shook his head again. "Shemuel, I cannot even guess."

The gabbai sighed. "We know," he said slowly, "that nothing in God's Word is written without purpose. This passage of Scripture has haunted me for years, my son. How I would love to ignore it, dismiss it along with others like it. But I cannot, Abiel, because many years ago something happened to me which makes it quite impossible for me to ignore this passage."

In Shemuel's eyes was a longing, an obvious desire to share something which troubled him greatly.

"Shemuel," the young man said softly, "what was it?"

"Ah." Shemuel smiled briefly; then looked at the floor for a moment. "You ask? I will tell you. About fifty years ago, Abiel, Herod was king in our homeland of Judea. Herod, as you know, ruled at the pleasure of Rome. I'm sure you remember much about him from your schooling, Abiel."

"I do, certainly," said the puzzled young man.

"Then you know this Herod was, oh, a baffling mixture of courage and cunning, daring and deceit. He curried the favor of the Greeks by building gymnasiums and amphitheatres.

They called him 'Herod the Great.' And for us Jews, well, he rebuilt the temple in Jerusalem which had stood since the days of Nehemiah. But did this prove him a friend of Israel? No, Abiel. Because, when the main gate of the temple was erected, Herod's true loyalties emerged—when he had a Roman eagle erected over it."

Abiel's face hardened.

"And when a mob of young Jews tried to tear the eagle down, Herod captured forty of them and had them burned to death." Shemuel's voice trembled slightly. "So it may be well that next time you go to the temple in Jerusalem, that you remember it was dedicated in Jewish blood."

"Why?" There was a hint of menace in Abiel's voice. "Why do you tell me this, and remind me of our slavery?"

"For this reason. Listen carefully, my friend. This Herod— we see how he went to such lengths to win the favor of his Jewish subjects. Yet we see how he was also utterly cruel in his loyalty to Rome. It was this Herod who, some fifty-five years ago, killed *every one* of the male children under two years of age in Bethlehem of Judea. Thereafter he was known forever as 'Herod the Wicked.'" Shemuel paused. "Abiel, you have heard of this atrocity, I know. But have you heard *why* Herod did this?"

"Weren't there rumors," Abiel said, "rumors that the Messiah had been born? And Herod sought to kill the young Messiah, if that could be possible. He was greatly mistaken, of course."

"Was he?" Shemuel smiled tightly at his friend.

"Shemuel! What are you saying?"

"I am saying that Herod was no fool. He was a master at the game of survival. Now think. After Herod went to such expense to win the favor of the Jews, would he have committed this atrocity in Bethlehem—which he knew would alienate them forever—unless he was convinced beyond all doubt that Messiah had been born there?"

Abiel knew at that moment a strange rising excitement, for Shemuel was touching the dreams, the hopes, the soul of every Jew who longed for the coming King.

The gabbai went on slowly as though unsure of how to proceed. "Abiel . . . I grew up in the shadow of that event, just as your father did. We grew up with the hope that maybe, just maybe, *Messiah was alive in the world!* Can you imagine the excitement of that? When I told you of the reason for Herod's massacre, you experienced a little of it, didn't you?"

"I did. Under your skillful unfolding of the past, I felt it."

"And then," Shemuel went on, "in later years rumors came constantly out of Palestine, rumors of an itinerant Nazarene prophet who could perform miracles, who could heal the sick and command unclean spirits. There were even very reliable reports that, on at least two occasions, he raised the dead back to life! All of that could only mean one thing, Abiel: that he was God."

"You believed this Nazarene could be the Messiah?"

"Yes!"

Abiel's voice grew hard. "I've heard of him, Shemuel, in my travels aboard ship. And I've heard of the demented people called 'Christ-Ones' who still worship His memory—for what reason I'll never know, because even they admit He was crucified. He was, wasn't He?"

"Yes," Shemuel nodded sadly. "He was crucified. And I was in Jerusalem the day it happened."

Abiel sat erect, his eyes as intent as a cat's.

"Yes. It would have been several years before you were born, Abiel. I was in Jerusalem for the Passover that year. The Nazarene, whose fame had gone before him, rode into the city in triumph on a donkey, the traditional mount of Jewish kings. The mob lining the street knew exactly what that symbol meant, and they were near hysteria in excitement. They waved palm branches for Him and shouted until they were hoarse: 'Hosannah! Save now!' They really thought the time had come. Really, Abiel, what better time for Messiah to appear than at Passover, when Jews from all over the world were crowded into Jerusalem? The city was gripped by a feverish excitement. Abiel, can you imagine what I felt?"

Abiel swallowed. "I'm feeling some of it now," he said

softly. In his mind's eye he saw Shemuel as a young man with his heart nearly exploding, his soul exulting in God.

"And so," Shemuel went on, "the Nazarene, named Jesus, went to the temple itself, just as you would expect. But there, instead of joining with the priests, He denounced them—called them hypocrites! He made a shambles of the temple worship that day, for He drove out the sacrificial animals and turned over the money tables; tables so heavy that even you, Abiel, would scarcely be able to lift one end of them. Yet they say He flipped them as if they were made of kindling sticks."

"So He was a madman," said Abiel.

"Well . . . that is a question being debated even today. But whether He was or not, He did not survive such effrontery. A week later He was hanging on a cross. The reason—because He plainly said He was the Messiah, the Son of God!"

"The Nazarene *claimed* to be Messiah?"

"Yes, He did. And so the Romans taunted Him—and us. They made a crown of thorn rose vines and jammed it on His head. That was His king's crown, they said. Then at the top of His cross they put a sign: 'This is the King of the Jews.' Abiel, I was literally sickened of body and soul. Needless to say, I left the scene. But . . . that scene has never left me." Shemuel sighed deeply. "It has haunted me through the years, just as this passage of Scripture written by David has haunted me. Abiel, we know that David wrote many passages describing what Messiah will do in His reign. Why then did David describe in such perfect detail what happened to that Nazarene? The executioners gambled for His coat, just as it was written a thousand years before."

Abiel knew at that moment a rising discomfort in his soul, a curious drawing of his spirit. Angrily he waved his hand as if to dismiss the subject. "Shemuel, surely you have considered that thousands of Jews have been crucified before and after this Nazarene! The fact He was crucified means nothing."

"Yes. But did the birth of any of those others trigger a massacre because they might have been the Messiah? Did any of them heal the sick or raise the dead? Did the sun go dark, and the earth tremble when they died? No!"

Unable to sit still, Abiel began to pace in the study, rubbing the back of his neck with one large hand. "Shemuel . . . you certainly agree He could not be the Messiah!"

"No, no, He could not be the Messiah. Because if He were, then where is He? He cannot rule the world if He is dead."

"Ah," said Abiel, relieved.

"And yet," Shemuel leaned forward in his chair, twisting his hands in obvious agitation, "Abiel, this mystery is very great. For, if the Nazarene was not Messiah, then who *was* He?"

As Abiel had stared into the troubled eyes of the gabbai Shemuel on that winter morning, he had the first inkling of the tragedy that would soon overtake Shemuel and his entire family—including Ruth.

Now, as he stood in the sun, leaning to the rudder bars, the aching void burned within him. It was loneliness and longing for Ruth, and it was rage toward the Nazarene deceiver, and Paul, and all like him.

CHAPTER 6

DAYS PASSED and the ship crawled, beating against the wind which blew steadily from the northwest with infuriating predictability. Even though they were frequently relieved by their first mates, both Abiel and Calliades gradually became exhausted by the constant concentration of steering a windward beat. Finally the two officers decided that, when they reached the Ionian port of Cnidus in a week or so, they may as well put in for the winter. The centurion was agreeable to that. So, of course, was the crew, who seemed to experience an immediate improvement in morale. Ah, the revelry to be found in Cnidus, they said, where there are temples to Bacchus, Diana, and Cybele, whose priestesses could satisfy a man's every desire. Abiel however, as usual, would live aboard ship with a caretaker crew and sleep before the warmth of the galley firepit. Every Sabbath he would go ashore to synagogue.

The only objection to the plan came from Lydas Phlegon, who accosted Abiel on the deck the next morning. "Ben Heled, you are thinking as woodenly as a Roman!" he whispered. "Look at this faultless weather, and think again of the money I would give you to continue on to Rome."

"The weather will not remain this way for long, Lydas. But if you are so determined to reach Rome this winter, perhaps you can find yourself another ship in Cnidus. If you can find a shipmaster reckless enough, you will deserve each other." Abiel's voice lowered confidentially. "And perhaps with any luck you could persuade the Romans to go with you."

That evening, Abiel and Calliades rotated their watches, and the day crew shifted to night duty. The ship was quiet as Abiel steered beneath the stars and a dim quarter moon. The wind had swung northward somewhat and, for a while at least, they moved fairly well. In changing, the wind had also become more variable, coming at the ship in radiating puffs called "cat's paws," and the men on the main deck below kept busy hauling in and letting out the sheets and braces in response to the whimsical wind. Yes, Farnaces and his watchmates were earning their money tonight.

With the rumble of waves at the bow, the swish of water aft, and the creaking of the yardarm, the *Athelia* swept along. In the weak moonlight her sails appeared to be suspended in the air as if by levitation, glowing white as though covered with frost. The softly shouted orders were ghost voices, and the ship was only a dim and passing mirage on the vast, empty sea. Abiel was happily absorbed in it, feeling the power of wind and water that pulsed through the rudders.

Up forward, a shaft of yellow light shot across the deck and vanished. Someone had emerged from the forward hatchway. There was nothing unusual in that except, a moment later in the dim moonlight, someone in a white cloak emerged at the deck stairs and came forward toward him. Abiel was a bit perplexed. Only a crew member would be coming to him on the aft deck like this; but no crew member wore a cloak like that, and no crew member moved like that. It was a woman. Abiel's heart quickened suddenly to see it was Demaris, and wordlessly he watched her come slowly as if in a dream.

"Captain? Ben Heled?"

"Yes . . . I am."

"Good. I gambled that it would be you. Forgive my rudeness, Captain, but are sleepless passengers allowed to come back here and talk?"

"Well, not as a usual thing."

"Oh." She paused, uncertain and, Abiel was sure, surprised. "Then I suppose I should go back."

"Wait." The word sounded in his usual tone of command, but tinged with an urgency he hadn't meant to be there. "I mean, is there a problem you need help with?"

"Actually, I'm a bit beyond anyone's help." She tossed her head slightly. "But my immediate problem is that I can't sleep. If you would let me break the rules and stay up here and talk a while, I'd like that."

"And," Abiel thought to himself, "so would I." He took a deep breath. "Then sit down on the rail step over there," he told her. There, at least, she would not be so conspicuous to crewmen on the deck below.

She sat down off to the side and rested her chin on her knees as she watched Abiel where he stood, his sharp face and beard silhouetted against the sky. "You seem to be working very hard," she said suddenly. "Will it bother you to talk?"

"For a little while it won't. I can steer like this in my sleep."

"It looks difficult." For a while she watched Abiel's smooth and measured movements as he worked the bars back and forth in time with the rising and falling of the wind. Obviously there was some silent teamwork here as well. Every few moments the yardarm swung, moved by unseen men on the deck below, responding to someone's muffled orders.

After a while Abiel became uneasy at her silent presence. "The idea is to keep the sail tight and smooth," he said. "My first mate, the proreus, on the deck down there watches the sail. If some wrinkles or creases come in it, he knows the wind has swung too far ahead. So they move it further fore and aft, you see. Of course, if the sail doesn't smooth out then, I must let her point away from the wind a bit."

"Hmm," she said. "You know, the ship seems to sway so much more up here."

"You should be on the platform atop the yardarm up there, if you really want to feel her sway."

"Well, it might be fun," she said unexpectedly. She was silent a moment. "Captain, do you know what I think?"

"About what?"

"About you."

He shrugged uneasily.

"Well, I've watched you steering, and I think you must be very strong and yet very gentle. And I think you must be a very good husband."

Abiel was a bit taken back. How brash and forward could this woman be? "I am not married," he said.

"Oh. I . . . I didn't mean to pry into your life, or anything. I only thought, since you are Jewish, you would be married." She lapsed into silence a moment. "Well then, Captain, did you know I am Jewish like you?"

"I thought perhaps you were. Most likely from Galilee."

"You're very observant." Her laughter silvered the air briefly. "My family did come from there, many generations ago. I knew you were Jewish, too, even before anyone told me. I knew it even before that big fight on the deck last week. Can you guess how I knew?"

"I suppose I look the part."

"You do. But I knew it as well from the way your ship is so clean, and the food is good. I was on a ship from Adramyttium once that had cockroaches as big as my hand." She faked a shudder.

"Well, we have a few ourselves," said Abiel. "But I insist on my men keeping things as clean as they can. It takes some of them a while to grow accustomed to the idea."

She laughed again. "I imagine so! It is so unusual. You're unusual."

"I've been told that before."

"I mean it as a compliment. I've never met anyone like you. I thought it was so dauntless when you wouldn't let the centurion share your cabin . . . because you obey God. And the way you make your crew behave . . . there is none of that obscene chanting when they're pulling on the ropes and such. It just seems to me it would require so much courage to be so different."

"We Jews have been different for thousands of years. You should know that."

"I'm afraid the Jews I've known haven't been very devout," she said. "Neither have I."

Abiel waited for her to continue, hoping she would tell something about her past—perhaps of how she had come to be a slave of Lydas Phlegon. Obviously, she had not been a conventional Jewish maiden trained to hearth and home. A woman of correct training would never have come so boldly to the captain, alone and at night. When she said no more, though, Abiel decided to ask indirectly. "Your master, Phlegon, is very upset we're stopping for the winter soon."

"Oh, let him be upset." An edge crept into her voice. "I care little if we ever see Rome. I would much prefer what I am doing now—being on the sea and talking to people." She pushed some windblown hair out of her eyes. "I *have* enjoyed being on your ship. Today was a wonderful day."

Her voice grew lighter as she told of the clouds of seagulls that had followed the ship during the day, and how, if she held up a piece of bread, they would swoop down and take it from her hand. "And then," she said, "there was another big grayish bird that started circling the ship this morning. It just kept circling, and went higher and higher until it was just a little speck in the sky. Finally it just disappeared—the way I would like to do sometimes."

"I saw the bird, too," said Abiel. "It is a kind of cormorant. We call them moon birds."

"Yes, that's what they called it."

"Seamen are superstitious about those birds, just as they are about everything else. If it comes back and circles the ship again tomorrow, that is an omen of good fortune. But if it doesn't come back, it means bad tidings for the ship."

"So tomorrow I suppose you will all be waiting with held breath."

"I won't," Abiel said. "But my crew will be watching for that bird, you may be sure. As I said, they are superstitious about everything."

"Do you chide them for it?"

"No. No, I don't. They live with some very powerful forces: wind and storm. And I've learned not to interfere with how they come to terms with it. For instance . . . oh, like the leather battens on the sail up there. If a ship has one batten made of hyena hide, that is supposed to keep lightning away.

So I have a strip of hyena hide up there just for the crew's sake. I don't believe it makes a bit of difference myself. And then, most seamen won't sign on unless you promise them there is a good-luck coin in the mast step." He cast a side-wise grin. "Nonsense things like that. But I don't chide them for it."

"And you honestly aren't affected by all of that?"

"No. I'm very sure the Master of the Universe does not need good-luck birds or coins to influence His will. I will leave those things to the pagans who have nothing better."

There seemed genuine awe in her voice then. "You speak as if God were real. I mean as if He were really known to you."

"Real?" Abiel paused a moment to think that statement over, and was surprised to hear himself say that, while God was undoubtedly real, He was not that well known to him. "It is like . . . like that star I'm keeping on the bowsprit there," he said painfully. "Night after night it is always there; and it is always true and dependable. But it is also so very far away. Very far away and . . ."

"Unreachable?" she asked softly.

He was silent a moment. "Yes," he said finally, "unreachable. It is the same with God."

She had gotten up and Abiel was a bit disconcerted to see and feel her presence close beside him on the other side of the rudder bar. Her voice, so close, was velvet. "Which star do you see to guide yourself, when the sky is so full of them?"

Abiel turned toward her. She was much too close; so close he could see her exquisite eyes slanted in the moonlight and smell her fragrance. His heart leapt. She was Ruth—Ruth standing so close to him on the rooftop in Alexandria that summer. He could only stare wordlessly as his heart tore. He wrenched his eyes away from her. "You should not be stand-ing here by the helm," he said. The tight excitement of his voice spoke volumes.

From below, Farnaces called out orders to tighten the star-board sheets.

"Belay that!" Abiel called. "We're off heading. Stand by."

The luff in the sail had come this time, not because of a shift in the wind, but because the captain had let the ship wander. Slowly the bow swung back until the yardarm crossed the Southern Star. Then the ship heeled as the sail billowed full again.

There was some disgust in the first mate's voice as he canceled his orders, and Demaris knew she was causing trouble. "I shouldn't be up here bothering you, should I?" she asked from her seat back at the railstep.

"Oh, probably you shouldn't," Abiel sighed. "It is just that—looking at you—it brought back a time from long ago, and I forgot what I was doing. That's all it takes to allow this boat to swing windward."

"Oh? Was it a time like this with another woman, Captain?"

Abiel paused, wondering why he would be talking like this, telling such things to a perfect stranger as though he had known her for years. "Yes, and with a girl I loved very much."

Demaris watched him a moment. His face was tilted upward stoically as he looked to his faraway, unreachable star. "Do you want to talk about her?" she asked softly.

"Well, there is nothing much to say. She is dead now, you see. And I am a Jew without a wife, a Jew without sons."

"I'm sorry to hear that. Did she die from a sickness, Abiel?"

"You may say that, yes." His voice grew suddenly bitter. "But it was not a sickness of the body, but of the mind and soul: a sickness which is creeping across the world like a dark plague. They say a principal carrier of it is aboard our ship on this voyage."

Into her voice came the underlying toughness he had guessed was there. "Captain, what are you saying?"

"I am speaking of the prisoner, Paul. Paul the Aged," he said evenly. "I am sure you have talked to him. You know he spreads this bizarre belief that a crucified Nazarene is the Messiah. I speak of *that* sickness."

"Then . . . you were not speaking of her *physical* death."

"No, but something worse." Abiel's jaw hardened in rising anger. Why was he *doing* this? On this beautiful silver night, why must his mind be forced back to such painful memories?

He had returned to Alexandria early that winter. As soon as possible he had left the ship and literally run up the Street of Kings, his heart bursting at the thought of seeing Ruth again. But instead of warmth and welcome, he had found the house of Shemuel cold and empty of furniture. Shemuel and his family were gone.

He had not been long in learning the reason. Shemuel, they said, apparently after years of contemplating the matter, had become a believer in Jesus the Nazarene. He had of course lost his position in the synagogue, along with his livelihood; thus he had been forced to sell his home. If the gabbai wished to embrace Jesus as the "Christos," they said, he should have done it secretly.

A distraught Abiel found the family in a neighborhood of menial tradesmen near the shipyards, where Shemuel was trying to build a trade as a wheelwright. Wiping sawdust and grease from his hands, Shemuel rushed out to greet his future son-in-law. Standing straight and tall, he looked healthier than Abiel had ever seen him.

Abiel was aghast that Ruth, whose beauty should commend her to a palace, was living in such a place. She ran to his arms and, as her youngest sister, Eve, danced excitedly around them, they embraced for a long moment. Yes, Abiel felt through her kiss, she was still the same as he had left her. He closed his eyes as his long voyage faded away and the cold sea wind retreated in her warmth. *Thank God*, Abiel thought. Yes, he would soon have her out of this squalid abode of pagans.

For Shemuel, though, he had only a forbidding gaze of scorn. "Do you consign your wife and children to this?"

"With food, clothing, and warmth we have enough," said Shemuel. And then his face lit up. "Abiel, what we have lost is nothing. Because I have found Him, the one for whom my soul cried. And I have found the mystery of the ages. Sit down, Abiel, please!"

But Abiel stood erect, looking at the old man as if he were a leper. "Is it true, Shemuel, what I've heard of you? Are you speaking of that dead Nazarene?" Abiel shook his head in disbelief. "What has happened to you? You may go to any burial ground and find a dead man!"

As Abiel's eyes swept the small silent room, a horror began to rise, replacing the numbness. Something in Ruth's eyes—was it pity for him? "Ruth?" he said incredulously. "Not you! May God have mercy!"

He was aware of Shemuel then beside him, laying a hand on his shoulder. "My son, we have all believed in Jesus the 'Christos'—Messiah! Please sit down and let us show you what we have found."

"You have found nothing but madness, and have infected your whole family with it!"

"No, not madness! The reason that Messiah had to die is the mystery of the Scriptures, Abiel. But He is no longer dead! The grave could not hold the One who is God Himself!"

This was utter blasphemy. With an explosive thrust of his arm, Abiel sent the older man staggering across the room into table and chairs; they toppled as Shemuel fell heavily to the floor. Hardly hearing the screams of the women, Abiel stood trembling. The anger drained as quickly as it had flared, leaving him in shock at what he had done.

"I'm well! I am all right!" Shemuel assured them as he rose slowly to his feet. But Abiel, as if in the presence of some great evil, began backing slowly toward the door. When Ruth left her father's side to run to him, he uttered the hardest words of his life. "No, no. Stay back. Don't you know it is unlawful for a Jew to touch the dead? Henceforth you are dead to me, and I to you."

His last memory of her had been as she reached to him in tears, her face twisted in grief. "But Abiel, I yet love you."

"Ruth was her name?" Demaris asked softly.

"Yes. Ruth," he said. "But it is done now. She is married to another—to a 'Christ One' as they call themselves. So it is done."

They were both silent for a while in the night. Finally Abiel spoke again. "I don't know why I tell you this, when I scarcely know you."

"And I scarcely know you either. But perhaps we will get to know each other better before this voyage is over." Her voice was gently inviting; and Abiel was surprised to feel a sudden wave of comfort and thrill that, for some reason, this woman seemed interested in him.

"Then, Abiel," she went on, "the one who hurt you is really the Nazarene, isn't it?"

"That is true," said Abiel slowly. "And now I am cursed to have aboard my ship the Nazarene's chief advocate."

"Paul." She nodded. "Many of us have talked with him since we left Myra."

"Oh?" Abiel growled.

"He is so convincing," she said thoughtfully. "Captain, please don't be angry at my saying it. And I don't know . . . I don't know enough of our Scriptures even to know if he is telling the truth."

"Those who do not know the Scriptures are his choicest victims."

"Well, it is very obvious that *you* know the Scriptures, and love them." She smoothed the hair back from her eyes. "I think you are a very good man, Captain, a righteous man— one of the few I've ever known. But I also think your right-eousness has made you lonely. And you have a deep, dark pain inside, just like everybody else in this world. That should not be."

"No," Abiel said softly, "it should not be."

"I only wish . . ." she sighed loudly; and the longing in it made Abiel's pulse increase. "I only wish I had known a man like you years before now. Perhaps I wouldn't bear the marks of a slave."

"Demaris, how *did* it happen that you should be a slave?"

"I'd rather not talk of it now, Abiel. The night is so beautiful, and we've had a good talk, haven't we? I'd rather just pretend I'm not a slave right now."

"Pretending can be dangerous," said Abiel.

When she didn't answer further then, a sudden annoyance crept into the captain's voice. "Perhaps you should go back and try to sleep now."

"Yes, perhaps I should. Maybe I will dream that I'm the moon bird, and fly away free." She laughed. "Captain . . . Abiel . . . may we talk like this again?"

Abiel thought a moment. Here he had revealed his deepest thoughts to this woman whom he didn't even know, and she had seemed to understand so well. Yet she, in turn, would tell him nothing about herself, so that he didn't even know who she was. There could be many reasons for her enslavement— some honorable, some not. Why then did he hear himself say that yes, they could talk again if she liked?

After she had gone and he was once again alone with the empty sea, it was easy to wonder if she had come to him at all.

CHAPTER 7

I CAN IMAGINE what it would be like to travel on a ship like that," Karen Chrisman said. "And I am very sure I would detest it."

Late into the night she and Robert Bonn talked. Outside Fabio's shed the wind had freshened from the east, and the booming surf had taken on an authoritative, ominous tone—a harbinger of the approaching storm. No longer was it Oberon's night. And yet, drawn by the presence of the ancient anchor submerged in the shallow tank, they seemed reluctant to leave it or each other.

"Well, didn't you enjoy the cruise you took last year? The one to St. Thomas?" asked Bonn.

"Sure, but oh, the difference!" She tossed her head and laughed. "That ship had casinos and bars, and theaters. And there was this marvelously handsome social director. But on a ship like St. Paul's . . ." Absentmindedly she reached into the tank to run her fingers across the old wood. "What was there to do? What could they *do* all day?"

Bonn grinned. "Talk, I suppose. Endlessly, and in great detail. Given some of the conflicts and tensions that must have been aboard that ship, I'd like to have some of those conversations on tape. And then I guess they spent a lot of time just thinking, you know? They would have had time to think deeply and logically about things. I'm afraid we've lost the ability to do that in our day—what with electronic games and TV, and people like your social director."

"Now Bob," she chided, "you're such a pessimist."

"Well, when is the last time you thought really *deeply* about something—say, the meaning of a person's soul?"

"That's right, Bob. Let's get serious here."

"See? But the people aboard that ship probably *had* time to think, and it was likely a real blessing. Of course, for some of them, it could have been a curse."

Directly beneath the aft deck, behind Abiel's cabin, was the cabin of Calliades the sailmaster. For sleeping Calliades preferred a hammock, which he had strung across the starboard side next to the porthole so he could lie and look up at the stars. A few feet away, on the port side, Julius the centurion had a pallet on the cabin floor. Both men were drowsy this night, and the centurion was drunk, as he had been on the past several evenings.

The distant rumble of waves striking the bow made for good sleeping. Over this sound was the rasp and squeak of the rudder shafts that ran through the sloping roof of the cabin. And if they listened carefully, they could hear another sound.

"She is up there talking to him again," said Calliades mischievously. "Listen hard, sir. I'm sure it's a woman's voice."

"She mus' . . . she must like your captain. Been going up there every night."

"And obviously the captain likes her," Calliades chuckled.

"She could awaken the love in any man—I tell you that," said Julius. They lay quietly, listening, but the voices came through only as muted tones. It was impossible to hear what they were saying, except . . . Julius raised up on one elbow. He was positive he heard the word *Caesarea*. The woman had said it, and he wondered what she could be telling Ben Heled about Caesarea. Not that it mattered, of course. He had nothing to be ashamed of for what had happened there. He listened awhile longer, then decided it was more likely he had not heard the word at all. No, more than likely he had only imagined in the recesses of his fogged mind hearing the name of that cursed place he wished he had never seen. And he reached for the wineskin once more.

"That's the trouble with me," he slurred to Calliades. "I've been thinking too much. Soldier isn't supposed to think. Just supposed to obey. Trouble is . . . there's nothing else to do but think. Jus' keep thinking and thinking over what happened in Caesarea . . ."

Julius had learned much about Caesarea Stratonis, the town built by Herod on the coast of Palestine. It was the headquarters for the Roman administration of Galilee, Judea, Perea and Samaria. When Julius arrived there for duty, the Roman procurator was a certain Antonius Felix. Normally, a procurator was a man to be envied. But this was not the case for Felix or any of his predecessors in the strange and baffling land of Judea. Not even the emperor Augustus had been able to keep a procurator in Judea for any length of time. Emperor Tiberius had fared a little better, his most successful appointee being a man named Pontius Pilate who survived in the office for ten years. But even Pilate had twice pushed the Jewish people to the verge of open rebellion. It seems that he, like the Romans before and after him, simply had not understood the Jews.

Pilate had arrived in Palestine with the firm belief that all these Jewish barbarians needed was some good Roman firmness to fall into line like everyone else in the empire. And why, he had wanted to know, were no Roman flags flying in Jerusalem? So one of Pilate's first decrees had been to order the flag of his legion flown in various places in the Holy City.

Unfortunately, these flags bore the image of the emperor—and at this point, Pilate had begun to learn the harsh realities of governing the Jews. It seemed these men worshiped an invisible God whose name they held in such reverence that they had no pronounceable word for it. This God had commanded them thousands of years before that they should worship no images. Obviously then, the emperor's image on a flag or otherwise could not be displayed in the holy city of Jerusalem. Thousands of Jewish zealots had descended on Pilate's headquarters in Caesarea, demanding that the flags be removed. In answer, the furious Pilate had ordered Roman

soldiers with drawn swords to surround the unarmed pro-
testers. Accept the Roman images, he had demanded, or be cut
to pieces. To his utter surprise, the Jews had silently bared
their throats to the swords.

One can only imagine what must have gone through Pilate's
mind as he saw the limits of power against the spirit of men
who worshiped God alone. The amazed and baffled procurator, with the power of Rome at his command, had backed
down, and the flags had been removed.

Pilate had learned from the incident but not enough. Years
later, when the Romans built an aqueduct into Jerusalem, he
had again stirred the Jews to rebellion by attempting to use
temple funds to pay for it. After all, he had argued, wasn't the
temple the chief beneficiary of this Roman engineering?
What did the Jews mean that the money belonged to God?
Pilate had fumed. Who could govern such incomprehensible
men?

Who indeed? Years later, the mad emperor Caligula, convinced he was a god, had made the same mistake and ordered
his statue to be erected in the temple. Jews by the thousands
had blocked the road with their bodies, perfectly willing to be
trampled to death rather than see the temple profaned. Just as
Pilate had done, the leader of the image-bearing expedition,
Petronius, had had to back down.

Didn't Pilate know? Didn't Caligula and Petronius know
that men who kneel only to God will never be subdued?

The procurator who had held the office prior to Felix was
Cumanus. The chief cause of Cumanus' downfall had been
his complete misunderstanding of the depth of religious
hatred existing between Jews and Samaritans. When he had
made a series of decisions that favored the Samaritans over
the Jews, the countryside had nearly erupted in civil war.
Rioting had become pandemic, and the situation in the rural
areas had deteriorated to virtual anarchy as guerrilla chief-
tains and bandits became the effective government. The emperor Claudius had been forced to remove Cumanus and, in a
move to pacify the Jews, had handed over Cumanus' assistant to be executed by them. It seemed that being a Roman

official in Judea could be not only exasperating, but also hazardous.

This was the situation when the tough Antonius Felix arrived to salvage the mess left by Cumanus. For a while it seemed he would be a successful ruler. He restored order to the countryside by capturing the guerrilla chieftain Eleazar and crucifying hundreds of villagers suspected of aiding him. Since most of Felix' atrocities were confined to the rural areas, the influential of Jerusalem were at first inclined to overlook them.

Julius Longidaneas might not have come to Judea at all, except that one of Felix' centurions fell sick and died. And Felix, when he applied to the legate at Antioch for a replacement, had certain specifications for the man he wanted. First, it had always been a source of irritation for Felix that the troops under his control were mostly Syrians and Samaritans recruited locally, and so he demanded at least a centurion from a real Roman legion—with combat experience. More important, Felix required a centurion who had never served in Palestine—who had developed no loyalties and had not yet been infected with the general madness of Judea. So into the quagmire of Judea came the relatively innocent Julius, for whom the only "right" was to obey the emperor, the only "wrong" to violate his oath and disobey.

At first he was not at all popular with Felix' Syrians, whose skills he found woefully below standards. The men groaned and muttered when, in spite of the heat of the garrison at Antonia, he began longer daily drill and weapons practice. But as the months passed, the troops' dislike of him grew into a grudging respect as their own self-respect grew. Their new commander was the kind of Roman they had heard about.

It was a pity then that, when the first test of Julius' troops came, it was a type of conflict for which Julius himself had no training or experience. In Felix' seventh year as procurator, a violent disturbance broke out in Caesarea itself, right under the nose of Roman authority. It resulted from an old rivalry. The Jews had always insisted Caesarea was a Jewish city because its founder, Herod, had been a Jew. The Syrians and

Samaritans strongly disagreed. There hadn't been a single Jew, they said, in the "old town" of Strato's Tower before Herod rebuilt it. And the fact that Herod had included such profane things as theaters and gymnasiums proved the town was meant for Hellenists.

This old festering quarrel erupted once more. What began as simple street fighting between Syrian and Jewish youths soon escalated into daily street battles between adults, using rocks and clubs as weapons. The magistrates tried vainly to stop it with arrests and whippings. Finally, since the Jews seemed to be winning, Felix decided it was time to send in the troops.

Julius' combat experience had always been against armed soldiers. Now he was faced with civilians in their own city, armed for the most part with sticks and clubs. Worse, like Cumanus, he had no idea of the depths of religious hatred that burned between Samaritan and Jew. Nor did he understand why Jews would fight for "their" land. He organized a simple pincers maneuver to catch the rioters by surprise and force them back into the Jewish section; he even led one arm of the pincer himself. That was a mistake, for the Samaritan soldiers and noncommissioned officers on the other arm of the pincer had no intention of heeding their commander's orders about "minimum necessary force." They took full advantage of the situation; Jewish blood flowed in the streets, and Jewish bodies piled up. Worse, the third cohort went wild in the Jewish quarter, breaking into private homes and businesses to pillage and loot.

After finally getting his men under control, Julius knew that much had gone wrong. Flanked by his aides, he rode down the streets; everywhere the sword and pilum had done their dreadful work. The bodies, mostly of young men, lay sprawled everywhere, their blood-covered mouths gaping in surprise. Julius rode past a woman and child dead in the street. Everywhere the wails of anguish and horror rose, but fell silent at the approach of Julius' group, for Jews would not cry in the presence of a Roman. When he passed, only the sound of the horses' hooves echoed eerily on the stones. One old woman kneeling over a body raised her head to gaze at the passing Romans. Her eyes never left Julius as he rode by, bathed in her silent hatred.

The centurion grew coldly angry. It wasn't the appalling number of casualties, or even the dead woman and child, that bothered him the most. After all, in Rome, not only was the rebellious slave crucified, but often his wife and children with him. No, the lives of those who disobeyed the emperor were cheap indeed. What bothered Julius was the looting by his troops—who were entrusted to enforce the law. These Samaritans had apparently never heard of soldier's honor.

Yet, as a practical matter, Julius knew he would be unable to identify and punish the individual offenders. Neither did he really want to, since he could not afford to have half his troops in the stockade at once. His solution was typically Roman and practical. He gave his troops a scathing lecture and restricted them to a diet of barley for a week—which was more a disgrace than a punishment to the soldiers. He also announced a coming inspection of the barracks and made it clear that any man caught with stolen goods would be punished. Julius was careful, however, to schedule the inspection far enough in advance to allow anyone with contraband to dispose of it. With that, his conscience was clear. He had satisfied the demands of justice within reason. The bodies in the street? Regrettable, but their blood was on their own hands . . .

Soon afterward, the new emperor Nero, wanting to appoint a procurator of his own, removed Felix and appointed Porcius Festus to replace him. When Festus arrived in Judea, he was met, as usual, with a lengthy list of complaints and demands from the Jews. First, they wanted the head of Saul of Tarsus— now called Paul—a religious teacher whom Felix had left imprisoned in Caesarea. Paul, they said, was trying to overthrow the law of Moses, was filling the world with strange teachings of a false Messiah, and had desecrated the temple in Jerusalem. A little further down the list, they also wanted the immediate trial and punishment of the centurion Julius Longidaneas, who had organized the "Caesarea massacre."

Julius had been utterly surprised when notified that Festus would hold a hearing on his handling of the Caesarea incident. The military lawyer appointed to represent him listened with a half-smile as, in his headquarters office, Julius paced slowly and resolutely like an actor on stage. With absolute confidence in Roman justice, he named the witnesses they should call in his defense—men who could testify that he had acted only in accordance with orders and regulations. He had been ordered to quell the rioting and had done so very quickly. Why then was he being charged with negligence?

"And why this outcry," his voice rose, "over a few Jews being killed? Weren't they resisting the emperor? Weren't they rioting in a city governed by Rome, and did they not refuse orders to stop it? Don't they know they are under Roman rule?"

The young attorney smiled. "Sir, I'm afraid that is part of our problem. You see, the Jews are *not* under Roman rule. Not really."

"And perhaps," Julius said coldly, "I should request counsel who can recognize a Roman flag?"

"No, sir. Please listen to me—for your own good. We govern Judea on papyrus perhaps, but *only* on papyrus." With that, the lawyer began recounting what someone should have told Julius long before then. He told of the utter ruin of every Roman official who dared tamper with the Jewish spirit, ending with the fate of Felix' predecessor, Cumanus. He told how Cumanus' assistant, Celer, had even been given to the Jews to be executed.

"They allowed the Jews to execute a Roman?"

"I cannot believe it, either, sir." The attorney laughed contemptuously. "Of course, Claudius would probably have sacrificed his own mother to buy peace in Judea."

Julius swore softly.

"I'm surprised no one has told you the real history of this place, sir."

Julius stopped his confident pacing and sat down slowly. "Well, I can understand now why Felix wanted a centurion from somewhere as far from here as possible."

"Sure. Someone who still had ideas in his head about Roman invincibility." The lawyer's grin vanished quickly at Julius' scowl. "Sir," he said quickly, "do you want to know who really rules Judea? Have you ever heard of the Jewish holy Scriptures?"

"Some, yes."

"Well, sir, *that* is what really rules Judea, in my humble opinion. It is a collection of ancient writings going back for thousands of years, which the Jews say came from their God Himself through His prophets. They've been carefully passed down. Their scribes even count the number of letters in the old and new copies to be sure not the slightest mistake is made in transcription. I'd wager, sir, that most Jews would gladly die in the defense of their Holy Scriptures. Now, it is these Scriptures, I've been told, which say that their God gave this land to their forefathers, and He spelled out the borders very clearly. As far as they are concerned, *that* settles the question of who owns and rules this land. We Romans are only temporary intruders, and they fully expect us to be driven out one day." The lawyer laughed. "Never has there been a race of people like the Jews. Never."

Julius was quiet a few moments, thinking over the strange and dismaying things he'd heard. "You said you were telling me this for my own good. Why?"

"Because, sir, I recommend you *not* defend yourself here in Caesarea. A fair inquest would be unlikely—and the Jews are after your head. I recommend you appeal to Nero's tribunal."

Julius' face went hard. "But I have done nothing wrong! Should I run from these people like a whipped dog?"

"Celer probably had done nothing wrong either!" snapped the lawyer. "Haven't I made it plain that *it doesn't matter?* If our courageous rulers were willing to sacrifice Celer, couldn't they do the same to you? Incidentally," the lawyer's voice softened, "do you know what the Jews did to Celer when they got him?"

"I have no idea."

"They dragged him completely around the city of Jerusalem. Then they took what was left of him and cut off the head."

Julius swore again, and suddenly he knew a sensation of empty desolation. He had known fear before, of course, but always when side by side with other soldiers of Rome who would die before they would retreat. He had always been backed by the honor of Rome, and with that, he could conquer any fear. Julius paced the tiled floor again, but more slowly now. His "caligae," soldier's boots, echoed in the atrium as he walked—boots that had never retreated.

"Now, I don't know yet what sort of man Festus is," the lawyer went on more softly. "I'm only saying don't press your luck by trying to vindicate yourself here. Why, even that leader of the Christians, Paul, recognizes the impossibility of a fair trial here. He has appealed to Caesar."

"Since when does a Roman follow the example of a Jew?"

"You see, sir, Paul may be a Jew, but he is also a Roman—*and* a doctor of the Jewish Scriptures, which the Jews accuse him of trying to destroy. Be that as it may, I know myself he is no fool. The other day he even had an audience with Festus and Agrippa, and they say he had them both trembling in their boots. Most important, though, Paul knows the mind of these people. Believe me, if he thinks he must appeal to Nero to survive, I suggest you follow his example."

Julius seemed to be wavering.

"Antonius Felix is in Rome now, isn't he?" the lawyer urged softly. "He could plead in your behalf. Weren't you in good favor with him?"

"I don't know if I was or not!" snapped Julius. "I didn't play that little game. I just did my job." The centurion paused and fixed with a contemptuous gaze this young smiling whelp whose sword had never seen blood. "You know," he said slowly, "I believe I am beginning to understand why you are so totally indifferent to my defense. Because it would really be to the benefit of Festus if I resigned my command and appealed to Caesar, wouldn't it? It would relieve Festus of the whole situation; he could wash his hands of the whole affair without offending his precious Jewish subjects. Festus would be most pleased, wouldn't he?"

The young man, leaning comfortably back in his wicker chair, met Julius' gaze with a sudden, casual contempt. His voice was cold when he said, "The centurion is at last beginning to understand. Yes, if you will appeal to Caesar, Festus will be *most* pleased."

Julius felt again the cold sickening dismay bordering on fear. His voice sounded strangely breathless. "I am to be relieved of my command, and I cannot count on the *procurator's* support?"

"The centurion is most perceptive." The lawyer's voice lowered. "Remember what happened to Celer. Forget your honor and your justice, and get out of Caesarea."

"I . . . I understand."

"I understand," Julius murmured as he stared into the darkness of Calliades' cabin. How strange that a man could grow suddenly older and die a little with the utterance of those two words. So much for the justice of Rome—in Judea anyway. So much for the courage of Julius Longidaneas. The Jews had done that to him.

Slowly Julius flexed his left hand and, as usual, a dull pain traveled through his forearm where the Parthian arrow had pierced it. The Parthians had been extraordinary archers. At full gallop on horseback they could hit a man a full stadium away, galloping in the opposite direction. Even against such fighters as that, Julius and Rome had prevailed. In the Rhineland with the Eighth Augustan, Julius and Rome had been victorious. But in Judea he had not been victorious. It was the Jews who had caused him to run when he had done no wrong, who had broken the iron code that had kept him fearless in the world. And he would never forgive them.

"Curse them all," he muttered. "Curse them all to the gloom of Tartarus forever—them *and* their God. Except . . ." Julius snorted, "they can't decide who He is."

Yes, here was Paul the Jew, traveling the world telling everyone that some other crucified Jew was God—and the other Jews were trying to kill him for doing it. Julius laughed aloud—a harsh, bitter laugh that awakened Calliades with a startled snore.

"So there is really nothing, is there?" said the centurion.

Calliades thought for a moment. "No, sir, I guess not," he said and rolled over, wishing this Roman wouldn't drink so much in the evenings.

"Nothing," Julius said again. "No Roman's god, no Jew's God." Alcoholic tears welled in his eyes as he lay back on the pallet. "Curse the Jews. Curse them all. But one day . . . yes, one day I will find the truth. Am I not a Roman? Am I not commander of . . . of this ship? So one day I will command them to tell me the truth."

After a few moments the centurion seemed asleep. Calliades, his prominent nose dimly outlined in the moonlight, looked with relief toward the Roman. "Romanos, rerum dominos, gentemque togatam," he murmured sarcastically. "Romans, lords of the earth, the race that wears the toga."

CHAPTER 8

OVER THE NEXT FEW DAYS the crew commented often on the curious change that seemed to be falling over their captain. The contrary wind seemed not to irritate him so much now. His brusque efficiency eased, and once he was seen to laugh out loud at a jest. Was it only coincidence, they wondered, that this mellowing should come at the same time the lovely slave woman began visiting him so often at night?

"I can hear them up there at the helm," Farnaces told his watchmates as they sat around the galley table. "Talking nice and low, and laughing sometimes. Very intimate if you ask me."

"Ah, my fellows," Calliades spread his arms expansively. "Can it be that love has at last smitten the rabbi?"

Abiel of course would have denied that. Yet, did not her buoyancy lift him whenever they met and brighten the long nights? Did not her forthright understanding comfort him? Did not the beauty of her hair and face and the soft outline of her breasts captivate him, her nearness make his heart race? Yet, for all of this, she remained like the faraway star—distant and unknown. For this reason, one night on the aft deck, Abiel became quite irritated and demanded she tell him of her past. Why was it that she, who was obviously not born to it, should be a slave?

"Abiel, why should it matter to you?"

"Because . . . it matters. That's all. It is beginning to matter more all the time."

"I'm glad it matters to you," she said. "Yet I almost wish it didn't, because we both know our friendship must end with this voyage."

"Perhaps. But it will be many months before we reach Rome, and I want to know who I am talking to every night up here. And it bothers me that you are ashamed to tell me."

"Abiel, believe me. There is no wrongdoing for me to be ashamed of. But it is just . . . just such a *sordid* story. Why must I demean myself?"

"Then you *are* ashamed."

"No, I am not."

"Then tell me."

She sighed heavily. Then, in a voice dull and tinged with flippant sarcasm, she began to tell how she had been the oldest and favorite daughter of an import merchant in the Judean coastal city of Caesarea. All her life she had indeed been accustomed to the best, and, as Abiel suspected, of generally having her way. The marriage her father had arranged with the son of a fellow merchant, however, had not been good. "My husband was the most selfish, irresponsible man I've ever known," she said. "And whenever he was drunk, which was very often, he would become quite sullen. He beat me frequently."

"I'm sorry your father did not choose more wisely," said Abiel.

She shrugged. "It wasn't his fault. My husband was very adept at deceiving people, and he could be so very charming when it suited his purpose. But when my father *did* learn of what was happening, he became enraged. He literally kidnapped me back to my home, where I would remain, he said, until my husband learned to behave better. As you can imagine, it caused quite an uproar in our quarter. To my husband's family it was unforgivable."

"I can imagine," Abiel murmured.

"But things became worse. My husband, to save face I suppose, began to accuse me of being a harlot and said he would give me a writing of divorcement. My father threatened to sue at law if he did, where he would demand proof and demand my dowry back. As I said, it was a very sordid thing. So we were all very surprised then when my husband became suddenly very conciliatory and charming once again. He made all sorts of promises of reform, you know. I went back to him, and my family thought things were settled. We didn't know of course his real reasons for taking me back." She took a deep breath. "His recklessness had put him deeply in debt, and his creditors were about to foreclose on him. He sold me to satisfy the debt."

Abiel's breath seemed to leave him. "Demaris, that is unbelievable! And your husband was Jewish?"

"No," she said. "As I told you, my family was not at all devout."

"May God have mercy on you," Abiel growled, "and consign your husband to the lowest pit of Sheol."

"That was my sentiment," she said dully, "until I learned that the bitterness was only hurting me, eating me from the inside out. And what bitterness it was, Abiel." Her voice caught. "I can't describe what it's like to suddenly find yourself on the same level as cattle and sheep. To be examined and stared at naked. Oh it was a wonderful revenge for what my father had done . . ." The aura of breezy toughness dissolved completely then as her shoulders began to shake; she held the wide sleeve of her cloak to her face and began to sob into it.

With the morning Calliades and his crew took over. Abiel held his usual morning conferences with the sailmaster and the two first mates. After breakfast, he retired to his cabin for some badly needed sleep, which he always found difficult to get in the daytime. Now, in his new turmoil of soul, he knew it would be impossible. Before bed, he lifelessly recited the morning "Shema": "Hear O Israel, the Lord our God is one . . ."

Then he thought to pray. But when the fringed prayer garment was in place, when the small leather Scripture boxes were tied to his wrists in the prescribed pattern, he found to his annoyance that his thoughts were not on God, but Demaris. With flowing grace she walked the deck in her white cloak. She stood close beside him at the helm, her lips parted, inviting, exhilarating—and heartrending.

"If," he thought to himself, "she could be *free.*" As he lay thinking throughout the morning, there suddenly dawned on him a plan whereby she might be. Excitement grew. Quite possibly it would work *if* he were willing to take a great risk. The only trouble was, the risk would be borne not only by himself, but by the innocent passengers who had trusted him with their lives. Somberly he weighed the chances of success against the possible wickedness of risking others for his own benefit. At last, irritable and sleepless, he arose and went out.

Already it was the noon hour of another brightly sunny day; passengers were eating as they lounged in scattered clusters on the deck and hatch roof. Only the ship's officers and crew could eat at the galley table. Nodding greetings, Abiel eased past the line of first-class passengers awaiting their meal from the cook and ducked into the cool shadow of the hatch entrance. Passing through the galley, he advised Plautus he would take his meal at the crew's table. Then, ducking through the bulkhead, he paused in surprise, for seated together alone at the table were the centurion and the prisoner, Paul.

The centurion looked up, seemingly pleased to see Abiel. "Ben Heled! We were hoping you would come to dinner about now. I planned this opportunity to talk to you and your fellow Jew here together."

Abiel drew up short. "That man is not my fellow in any sense of the word. And do you bring prisoners to the captain's table?"

"As commander of this ship I bring him," said Julius. "It happens that Paul is instructing me. Ben Heled, I would like very much for you to join this conversation. Sit down. Please."

Abiel, now recovered from his surprise, shook his head slowly. "No, I will not defile myself by listening to heresy. But you . . . feel free to continue. I am sure this charlatan would like to count a centurion among his victims."

"Just a minute!" Julius' voice rose in irritation. "You say he is a charlatan. Then for what gain? Don't you see it has earned him nothing but a prisoner's chain?" The centurion caught Abiel's eye. "No, Ben Heled, I am not that naïve. I believe there is more to Paul's belief than deception—and I believe *you* are afraid of what it may be."

A curious burning rose in Abiel's chest. Why indeed had Shemuel and Ruth given up everything to follow the Nazarene—and done so joyfully? "I do not know what it may be," he said finally. "Let Paul answer for his own folly."

"And how will I know it to be folly unless someone learned in your Scriptures is here to dispute him? You, however, are afraid to do it."

Abiel studied the centurion's drink-swollen eyes. "Why? Why do you care?"

"Because if I am to be defeated by the Jewish God, I want to know who He is."

"There is no question as to who He is," said Abiel slowly. Walking over to the porthole, he opened it. "With your permission," he said wryly. "The stench of lies makes me ill." Taking his seat at the table, he glared at Paul, then smiled sardonically. "Then what has Paul told you of his Nazarene?"

"Paul may speak for himself," said the centurion. "And now, Paul, will your words be so bold in the presence of another Jew who knows your Scriptures?"

On the face of the urbane and spry old man was that same look as when Abiel had first seen him—a sure peace and joy, as if buried within him was some wonderful secret of life. His smile was utterly compelling, and his voice—that of the trained orator—easily filled the cabin. "I have given my defense before the rulers of the Jews, and I have given it before the procurators of Judea, both Felix and Festus. Now, I will most gladly give it before this worthy son of Abraham. Ben Heled, will you indulge me?"

"It seems I have little choice."

"Then let me emphasize, it is from the Scriptures alone— the Scriptures we both love—that I have instructed the centurion here. I have shown him how, from the beginning of our nation, God's prophets have foretold the coming of the Righteous One who will be the Savior of Israel. Indeed, He will be the Savior of all mankind. I told him of how there are hundreds of passages, written over thousands of years, that give glimpses of Messiah's coming and His eternal reign over all the earth. But the passages are often in obscure and shadowy context; they appear like pieces of a puzzle given by God to His prophets. Do we agree, Captain, that this is true?"

"Of course. And I look forward to their true fulfillment, as you should."

"If you truly await Messiah's appearing, you are blessed of God," said Paul softly. "Then hear me carefully, Ben Heled. I have shown the centurion how the pieces of this puzzle find their resolution in only one man—Jesus of Nazareth."

Abiel stiffened. "Here is the lie."

"Not a lie," said Paul intensely. "Did not the prophets write that Messiah will be born in Bethlehem of Judea and be a descendant of King David? Did they not write that He would enter Jerusalem in triumph on a donkey, and that He would be valued by a friend at thirty pieces of silver? This is all true of Jesus. Even His crucifixion, Ben Heled, was foretold in detail! Surely you have read the Psalms."

"Enough! Do not mouth the heresy—could *God* be crucified?" Abiel swallowed hard, for, in his mind's eye, he saw that rainy day in Alexandria when the gabbai Shemuel had read from his scroll: "I am poured out like water and all my bones are out of joint. . . . They pierced my hands and my feet. I can count all my bones . . . "

"I have read the Psalms," Abiel glared at Paul, his eyes burning. "And I know such words were written by David. But by what *right* do you say he was speaking of Messiah? Could God be crucified? Could God die?" The shipmaster's clenched knuckles were white. "It is blasphemy! Blasphemy of the worst kind!"

Abiel's anger was more effective than his words. The centurion looked at Paul, questioning. "Very well. Answer him, Paul. If this Jesus was the Messiah, then why did such a horrible thing happen to Him? Paul, can't you see the absurdity of that?"

"Absurdity?" Paul smiled down at the tabletop for a moment. "No. Because Messiah came to set Israel—and all mankind—*free*. Did He not?"

"From the tyranny of Rome," Abiel snapped.

"No," said Paul. "But from a tyranny far worse—the tyranny and curse of sin! Gentlemen, listen! In two days we celebrate the Holy Day of fasting, the Day of Atonement. On this day, the high priest of Israel takes an animal, a scapegoat, and symbolically he lays upon it the sins of all Israel to be borne away. Abiel, is this not true?"

"You know very well how we celebrate the Day of Atonement," Abiel growled.

"Then," said Paul, "must we not look beyond the mere ceremony to the deeper meaning of it? Can a mere animal take away sin? Could a mere animal atone for wickedness? Or is this ceremony only a foreshadowing of when the *real* Sin Bearer will appear?"

There was silence in the cabin except for the rasping of the rudder shafts and the mewing of seagulls that floated through the open porthole. Then Julius' eyes lit with a sudden understanding. "So you are saying that *Messiah* is somehow the Sin Bearer?"

Paul beamed. "Yes."

"It could not be!" Abiel rasped.

"Abiel, my brother," said Paul. "That He would bear the sins of Israel was foretold along with the rest of it. Who else could the prophet Isaiah have been speaking of when he wrote these words: 'He was wounded for our transgressions, He was bruised for our iniquities: the chastisement of our peace was upon Him; and with His stripes we are healed. All we like sheep have gone astray; we have turned every one to his own way; and the Lord hath laid on Him the iniquity of us all'?"

Abiel smoldered. He had never heard this passage of Scripture before. "But whoever Isaiah was describing, it could not be Messiah. Whoever David described as being crucified could not be Messiah. One does not rule the world from a cross!"

"Precisely!" Julius interrupted. "Here is the impossible contradiction, Paul. If your Messiah died—as a Sin Bearer or for any other reason—then how can He rule the earth?"

"Ah," said Paul. "Don't you remember I've told you before? Having conquered sin, Jesus also conquered death! Can't you grasp what I am saying? He came back to life again. He literally came out of His tomb! And, in so doing, He proved it all. He proved He is God forever."

In the centurion's heart arose an unexplainable burning, a tugging sensation he had never experienced. This was the key, he felt. He was close to the thing which would unlock the puzzle—if it were true. And, in spite of his fog of anger, Abiel's mind went back to that day when Shemuel had said the same monstrous thing—that the Nazarene had come back to life.

"Paul!" Julius said. "Is there proof of that? Proof?"

"Proof?" Paul said. "You are speaking to one who has seen Him. With my own eyes I saw Him. With these ears I heard Him speak."

The cabin erupted then as both Abiel and Julius began talking at once. A hound on the scent, the centurion rudely waved Abiel to silence. "Quickly!" he snapped at Paul. "*Where* did you see Him? *How?*"

"It was about thirty years ago," said Paul. "And where? On the road that runs from Jerusalem to Damascus. Nine deputies were with me who saw what happened. None of them ever disputed my account."

"Nine deputies?" Julius' eyebrows raised. "What sort of deputies?"

"It may surprise you to hear," Paul said slowly, "that thirty years ago I was commissioned by the highest Jewish court, the Sanhedrin. My task was to arrest, kill, wipe out those who believed in Jesus the Nazarene."

Abiel felt his heart grow cold in the sudden realization that he might be against something bigger than he had supposed. "*You* were commissioned by the Sanhedrin?"

"Very briefly," said Paul. With that he gave the shipmaster a look of such compassion that Abiel could not take his eyes away. "That is why I understand the anger boiling in you now," Paul said softly. "I once knew it myself against the Nazarene and His followers. Just like you, I loved God passionately; and when I first heard of Jesus, I was filled with righteous anger just as you are. I even helped kill the first of the Christian orators, a man named Stephen Ben Tobias—and I killed many more after him."

"And you were going to Damascus for *that* purpose?"

"Yes. Many Christ Ones had fled there from Jerusalem, you see." Paul looked past Abiel, out at the bright sunlight reflecting on the ship's varnished railing. It seemed he was looking far away. "It was a six-day trip, much of it across desert. There was the silence, and the stars so close at night just as they are here on the sea. I remember how, like a wayward ox, I was kicking against the goad of my conscience. I could not forget the face of Stephen, which shone like an angel's when he made his defense before the Sanhedrin. I saw that face in the sun and in the campfire at night. I couldn't forget his brilliant arguments, or the way he had died. Because he died calling on Jesus to forgive *us*—the very ones who were pounding him to death with stones.

"And so, along about noon that day, we saw Damascus there like a jewel in the desert. I urged my men on. Like a leopard I was closing in on my prey, and I thought if I could just be about my work, the doubts in my mind would vanish. And then suddenly . . ."

From force of habit, Paul held out his arm in orator style. His chain hung like the folds of a toga. Wonder filled his voice. "Suddenly a shock shivered through the air. A tremendous bright light hit me—so bright that even the Syrian sun dimmed to copper. It literally knocked me to the ground, along with my deputies. And in this numb shock of terror, I heard a voice speaking in Jewish Aramaic, calling what at that time was my name. 'Saul! Saul! Why are you persecuting me?'"

The old man paused. Abiel's face was hard and expression-less, while the centurion's was intensely alert. Neither man could take his eyes off Paul.

"I knew Who was speaking," Paul went on softly. "But I asked Who it was anyway, even though my voice would hardly come out of me. At the same time I looked up—and I saw Him with my own eyes, in His risen eternal glory. I saw Him! Jesus, the one I was persecuting."

"A mirage? A mirage in the sun?" Julius asked weakly.

"No," said Paul. "For I was blinded by His glory for days afterward. A person is not blinded by a mirage, nor are ten men knocked to the ground by one."

"Then what did He say? Surely there is more."

"Oh yes, He said more." Paul's voice clouded. "And He said it with such a tenderness and love as I cannot forget. 'It is hard for you, isn't it,' He said, 'to kick against the goad?'"

"He knew!" Paul went on. "He knew the agony of my soul, how I wanted so desperately to please God. He knew it all. And I can tell you that from that day my life has belonged to Him. I am His bondslave, and I will gladly be so to the end of my days—even though it has earned me nothing but this chain."

The centurion was breathing hard. A judge of men, he knew perfectly well he was not listening to the tale of a lunatic. Rather Paul, this cultured, learned man, knew what he had seen and had told it with perfect clarity.

Abiel shook his head abruptly and silently cursed himself. He had listened for so long to this deceiver that he was in danger of being seduced himself. His back straightened. "One may see many things on the desert," he said, "and embellish the story through years of repeated telling. But what *proof* have we really of what Paul saw, if anything?"

"The fact that I, once a member of the Sanhedrin, now sit before you with this chain?" asked Paul. "Is not that proof?"

"No," Abiel swallowed. "It is certainly not proof of your sanity."

"Very well, Captain," Paul said slowly. "Of the men who

were with me when it happened, some are still living. Unfortunately, none are aboard this ship to give testimony. There is, however, a third proof. But you may have to wait to see it."

"Wait?" said Julius. "Then we will wait! Go on. Tell us what the proof will be."

"There is a group of men," Paul said, "who were with Jesus when He lived among them on earth, all of whom saw Him *after* His rising from death. These men are called apostles— 'special messengers.' To attest to that status, and the fact they had seen Jesus alive after his resurrection, they were given certain abilities; for instance, the power to heal disease and the ability to receive direct revelation from God, just as our Jewish prophets of old. And I, as an apostle born out of due time, as it were, have been granted these abilities. They attest to the fact I have seen the risen Messiah, the Christos."

"Then," said Julius tightly, "here *is* proof. May we see . . . ?"

Abiel, too, his throat dry and pulse throbbing, leaned forward, afraid of what might come next. The tension in the little cabin was oppressive. But Paul only leaned back wearily in his chair. "No," he said. "I will not entertain you as one who pulls cobras out of wicker baskets. Because the truth of who Jesus is must be perceived by the spirit."

Julius sighed. For Abiel, the pressure in his chest lightened. He smiled wryly and quite suddenly was glad he had faced this deceiver. "Then let it stand," he said, "that what you saw was only a mirage in the desert." With triumph in his eyes he looked toward the Roman. "Let it also stand that this Jesus could not be Messiah, for the simple reason He is not reigning on the earth. Did He rise from death? Then where is He? He is keeping Himself well hidden for one who is supposed to rule mankind."

Julius, his excitement waning, looked to Paul. "That is true, Paul. Why is He not reigning?"

Paul eyed them both directly. "There is coming a time when He will return to earth a second time—to reign. And every knee in heaven and earth will bow to Him. But, Ben Heled, He is *not* ruling as king now. Do you know why?"

"Because He is *not* the king."

"Ah!" Paul caught Abiel in a somber gaze. "You have spoken truthfully, Ben Heled. He is not your king, because Jews such as you prefer your own righteousness to the righteousness of God. You prefer your own approval to the forgiveness provided by God, and you rejected the One sent to be your Sin Bearer. And because Israel rejected Him as Sin Bearer, He will not now reign as king."

At that, the anger rose in Abiel like boiling water. Slowly he got up and rose to his full height, towering over them both, his lips so drawn that white showed around them. "All of my life," he said, "I have kept the commandments of God. All of them! I have worshiped no idols. I have killed no one. With whom have I committed adultery? I have not sinned! I have given up the woman I love because I love God more!" He pointed toward Julius. "I have incurred the anger of this Roman because I fear God more. How dare you accuse me of rejecting the Messiah? I have lived my whole life to bring Him to earth!"

Abiel's voice rose so it rumbled like thunder in the close confines of the cabin. "I have no *need* of your Sin Bearer. *I have not sinned!*" Then, with one final glare at Paul, both of menace and triumph, Abiel marched swiftly from them.

Paul followed with his eyes and sighed deeply. "You know," he said to Julius, "once I spoke at Mars Hill in Athens. The Athenians listened very politely, just as they will listen to anyone. Then they just smiled and walked away. No anger or debate. They just walked away. How devastating that was! I much prefer a man like Ben Heled; one who has enough regard for God that he can become angry." Paul looked suddenly to the centurion, his eyebrows raised in good-natured questioning. "And what do I have from you, sir? Anger? Or belief of my report?"

"You have my respect," said the centurion slowly. "I know you are telling what you are convinced is true."

"And . . . ?"

Julius sighed. "Paul, it seemed for a moment there I was getting so close to the truth of it all. But . . . Ben Heled is right, is he not?" If Jews like him have not sinned, they did not *need* a Sin Bearer. So there is no pretext for the Messiah's failure to reign."

Paul smiled enigmatically. "*If* they, or you or I have not sinned. But the whole law of Moses is there to show us we indeed have."

"Ben Heled vigorously disagrees."

"I pray one day Ben Heled's eyes will be opened to see what the law is really saying," Paul said softly.

The centurion sighed. "When you told of the Nazarene's rising from death, I thought we were drawing close to the truth, perhaps. But no. The truth of all this is, for me, like the wind—not to be grasped, out there in the sun."

"Well." Karen laughed to her friend on the sultry summer night—now turned ominous and foreboding. "You're making them seem more human all the time."

"So they're coming to life out of the bas-relief carvings?" Robert grinned.

"Yes, they are. Okay. So then tell me why your shipmaster was so reckless? He should have stopped at Cnidus for the winter. Why did he sail across the open water to Crete if it was so dangerous?" She listened for a moment to the rising surf, drumroll of the approaching storm. "And I can see why it *was* dangerous this time of year. And why didn't he listen to Paul's warning later on?"

Bonn shrugged slightly. "I once knew a really devout Jew, like the shipmaster, and I don't think either man would be reckless at all. I don't think the shipmaster *could* have been. But . . . given the circumstances . . . if you use your imagination, you can come up with some pretty good reasons for what he did."

Striding back to his cabin, Abiel encountered Calliades' first mate, a red-haired boy from the Taurus Mountains named Pasher. "Sir," he called. "Calliades says he recognizes the coastline. We should see the port of Cnidus any time now."

"Call me when the lookouts spot it!" snapped Abiel; and,

disappearing into his cabin, he slammed the door. Inside, he held for a moment the small leather boxes of Scripture in his palm. Then, in an act which would shock any Jew, he flung them violently against the bulkhead. *Why?!* his soul screamed. Why did David write such ridiculous passages about a crucified man? Why did Isaiah write so mischievously of a Sin Bearer? Did God have such a perverse sense of humor that He would put such riddles in His Scripture? There were just enough riddles for deceivers like Paul to seize upon and mock those who truly sought to serve God. Of what use indeed was there in walking righteously and waiting endlessly for a promised Messiah who never came?

It was then that the thought of Demaris flowed over him like a soothing balm, and he thought again of his plan to set her free—a plan that would involve much risk. But why should he forever weigh his actions in the balance of right and wrong and deny the cries of his own heart? In this dangerous frame of mind, he went looking for Lydas Phlegon.

He found the slave merchant in the men's passenger area where, with sea trunk, pallet, and locker, Lydas had marked out much more than his share of space. Seated on a cushion atop the trunk, with his back against the slanting hull, Phlegon was reading *The Satyricon*. He seemed mildly amused that Ben Heled would request a word with him in private.

In the passageway beneath the lamp, they paused as Abiel looked to be sure no one was nearby. "Okay, Lydas," he said, his voice low and tight, "how much is it really worth to you to reach Rome by winter?"

Lydas' eyes opened with restrained sarcasm. "My boy, I offered you a handsome incentive, which you refused. It was beneath your righteousness, or some such nonsense, to risk . . ."

Abiel abruptly waved him to silence. "None of your wit, Lydas. I will make you an offer, and all I want from you is a yes or no. I will deliver you and your money to Rome—to the port of Puteoli—by winter. In exchange," Abiel took a deep breath, "you give me ownership of Demaris."

Lydas seemed floored. "My boy! I did not think good Jews like yourself kept slaves."

"What I do with her is my business. The only thing I want from you is your answer. Yes or no?"

They were silent as a passenger passed them on his way to the deck. Alone again, Phlegon appeared in deep thought. "My client in Ravenna would be most disappointed, of course. And yet . . . Ben Heled, could you have me in Puteoli by the Feast of Saturnalia?"

Abiel swallowed. "It will involve some risk, Lydas. With this headwind as it is, I will likely have to tack south around Crete. But, yes, I will have you there by Saturnalia."

Phlegon nodded slowly. His bulbous eyes narrowed as across his face crept the bland smile of success. "Then it is agreed. For obvious reasons, Captain, we should tell no one about this. Not even the woman."

"Obviously. You wouldn't want the other passengers to know I was taking risks just for your benefit, would you?"

"And for yours as well; so save your righteous indignation, Ben Heled." The bland smile returned as Phlegon turned to go. "Fulfill your end of the bargain, and she's yours."

CHAPTER 9

*I*MMEDIATELY ABIEL LEFT PHLEGON and ascended the steps to the aft deck, where Calliades of Rhodes wrestled their ship against the wind. The sailmaster was tired but enthusiastic as he gestured toward the faraway coastal ravines. "I know this land, Skipper," he shouted. "We'll see Cnidus before dark, or I'm one of Marius' mules!"

"Yes, Pasher told me Cnidus is coming up," said Abiel. "But it seems we're getting there much faster than we planned, don't you think?"

Calliades swore. "You're jesting! I feel like I've waded through the Styx waiting for that port to show up!" Then he slapped his knee and whooped. "But we'll soon be wintered there, Skipper, and we'll have a time."

Abiel looked down and grimaced. "Look, Calliades, let's not kid ourselves. The weather has been perfect the last few weeks, and it shows every sign of continuing thus."

"Uh oh." Calliades cast a sidewise glance at his younger captain. "What are you thinking about, Abiel?"

"I am thinking it's foolish to put in for the winter when the weather is safe for sailing."

"Safe! Sure," rasped Calliades. "But I'll tell you something. With a west wind like this, we're not going any further. We're just beating ourselves to death and getting nowhere. So why not put in to port and give everybody a rest?" His voice became conciliatory, a technique at which Calliades was a master. "Abiel, we can't change the wind. Even a Jew can't work miracles."

"Who requires miracles?" said Abiel evenly. "I've been thinking the last few days . . . Crete should be to the southwest of us. With the weather this good, what would be wrong with a southern run around Crete?"

"I was afraid you would think of that," said Calliades. "I really was."

"Well, isn't it reasonable? We'll head southwest toward Crete. That heading will put the wind on our starboard beam, and we'll reach Crete in two days easily. Once in the shelter of it, we will head west again. And then," Abiel went on as if he had just thought of it, "if the misbegotten wind is still blowing from the west, we will just tack north toward Greece, eh?"

While Abiel talked, Calliades released the bar to stroke his beard stubble thoughtfully. Both men had at their disposal only a general idea of the directions and headings, distances, and times needed to accomplish a plan like this; the guidebooks were of little value once away from coastal landmarks. "It's risky," said Calliades morosely. "There is always that little string of islands we would see if we drifted too far east . . . if the visibility stayed good. But I'll tell you one thing, Abiel. I don't like crossing the open sea to Crete this time of the year."

"But doesn't the sky look good?"

"Well, there's no bad weather around *now*," Calliades admitted.

"Let's head her south then."

"You know, Abiel, this isn't like you. You're scaring me."

The captain became irritated. "We'll be across in two days at the most!"

"Sure!" Calliades' voice rose. "Assuming our navigation is good! Assuming no storm blows up like it should this time of year. It is only a day before the Fast, Skipper."

"I know what day it is, and I have no intention of risking the ship."

"What Captain on the bottom ever did? And I'll tell you something else," Calliades shook his head and grinned sardonically. "The crew will want to scourge you."

"Can't say I'd blame them."

Not long afterward, the lookout atop the mast platform sighted the columns of Bacchus' temple at Cnidus gleaming in the low sun. Now sure of their position, Calliades had his first mate break the news to everyone as gently as possible. Soon the *Athelia* began turning south as Pasher of Taurus and his men hauled the great yardarm around. The men were grumbling and would not meet the eye of their captain, who was pointing the bow away from the taverns, the temples—and safety.

With a strong wind now coming from slightly aft of the starboard beam, *Athelia* heeled to port and began to pick up speed; the slap of waves at the bow grew to a muted thunder. After the long days of crawling, beating into the wind, Abiel found the speed exhilarating. His enthusiasm obviously was not shared by the crew and some concerned passengers, however, as they watched land slowly receding in the distance behind them.

The centurion was on the aft deck almost immediately. "Captain, what are you doing?"

"It was my understanding you wished to make haste to Rome," Abiel rumbled. "With the weather as good as it is, we would be foolish to stop now."

"But . . . Rome is not southward."

"Ah." Abiel nodded, then cooly began to explain his strategy of one great tack against the west wind—southwest to Crete, then west in the shelter of the island, then back northwest again to the Greek islands. "Believe me," he concluded, "with the wind as it is, this will be the faster way to Rome."

"But your men are grumbling over this new course, and some of them seem apprehensive. Why?"

Abiel paused. "There could be danger in the open sea this late in the year—for the careless. But the sailmaster and I both have examined the sky and waves for signs of bad weather. There is none nearby."

The centurion searched Abiel's face while Abiel steeled himself, aware this Roman, with one word, could wreck his plans for Demaris.

"And you are not being careless, Captain?" Julius murmured.

"Would I endanger my own ship?"

"No," the centurion said thoughtfully; and a slight grin crossed his face. "And, of course, Captain, I assume it is in your Jewish law that you should not endanger innocent passengers."

Abiel swallowed, his throat drier than he wished. "You are correct in that."

"Good. Then let me make two suggestions. You should address the ship's company and explain why we have changed direction away from land. And next time, Captain, be sure you consult me first before making any such changes. Have you forgotten I am in command?"

"How could I forget?"

The centurion glared at him a moment, then turned on his heel toward the deck steps.

That night Demaris came again as Abiel stood watch at the helm. After the tearful evening before, when she had recounted her descent into slavery, it was good to see her again chipper and defiant—and changeable as the wind. She laughed about the consternation among her fellow passengers over the course change, and in the next breath was concerned about the rumors of danger.

It was obvious to Abiel that Phlegon had told her nothing. She had no idea the change in course had been for her. All that night, he wrestled with the question of whether or not to tell her. There were dangers in her knowing. Yet, she must be told, he decided finally, simply because he had one great question for her, and he could not rest until he knew her answer.

The night grew colder than usual. Anxiously he awaited the dawn. Carefully he watched the sunrise for any signs of brewing storm, for his ship was yet a day from land and alone on the endless sea. A touch of pink glowed in the eastern sky, then the faintest tinge of yellow; but the glowering red hues he would have dreaded to see did not appear. Yes, weather to the west was good. Relieved, he murmured his thanks to the Master of the Universe.

Restlessly Abiel waited until breakfast. Then, while most of the passengers stood in the breakfast line, their cloaks wrapped tightly against the morning chill, he found Demaris and asked her to come with him to the forward passageway, one of the few places they could have any privacy. There he told her why the ship had changed course. How difficult it was for Abiel to keep his voice steady as her eyes widened in questioning surprise. "You see," he murmured, "I have made a covenant with Phlegon. I will see to it that he arrives in Puteoli by the Feast of Saturnalia. In return, he will give me ownership of you." His heart pounding, he carefully watched her face.

The edges of her beautiful mouth twitched upward and the exquisite eyes nearly closed as if in pain. "Abiel, I will awaken and find this is a dream."

"No. It is most surely not a dream."

"Abiel . . ."

"And when you are mine, I will set you free. You will be able to return to Caesarea, or do whatever you like. Or . . ."

She took both of his hands, and it was so natural for Abiel to draw her to himself, to press her warm lips to his while one big hand caressed the softness of her hair. They stood thus for a moment, lost in the happiness and smoldering excitement that flowed between them. "Abiel, don't ever bid me leave you. I would die," she murmured.

"I think . . . so would I," he said. "Oh, Demaris, that is what I wanted so desperately to hear you say. Because I love you—more than I did Ruth, more than I thought possible."

She stared at him, breathing through parted lips. "I love you, Abiel."

How bright was the morning after that as the sun sparkled in a thousand diamonds on the choppy waves. The world was alive. And Abiel was alive with a curious mixture of exhilaration and tension—the way a man feels, he supposed, when he has wagered all he owns on a throw of the dice. In his cabin for some much-needed sleep, he found it impossible. He tried eating a little lunch, then roamed the ship. A short conference with Calliades revealed that Crete was not yet in sight. There was no reason yet to be worried, of course, but Abiel climbed the mast to the lookout platform.

Big Naso was on duty there, sitting with his back against the mast. "Still no sight of Crete, sir," he said as Abiel poked his head through the hatch.

"We should be seeing it soon," said Abiel as he climbed through. For a while he stood on the platform, one arm hooked through the mast rope, and scanned the southern horizon.

The *Athelia* was plowing through choppy waves which themselves were riding atop a very soft swell. From the deck, the ship's roll and pitch was hardly noticeable; but up here the mast swayed as the horizon surged slowly up and down. For a while Abiel enjoyed the wind and clean air and the wild freedom of it. He relived the morning rendezvous with Demaris and saw her face in the sun.

Suddenly then, as the mast swung past its high point, he noticed the faintest disturbance of vision on the horizon ahead. Like a dancing heat wave, more sensed than seen, it tantalized the eyes. Abiel knew it would not be long until the mirage condensed into solid land, as though being created before his eyes. A renewed surge of exhilaration swept through him. "Crete," he said to Naso. "Thank God. Stand up here where you can see better; see if that isn't land ahead."

Naso agreed. Soon, with a light heart, Abiel descended the mast ladder to tell Calliades. "But you had better steer more eastward," he laughed, "because it looks like you're hitting it amidships. We should be there by tomorrow's dawn."

The two men laughed together. There was nothing funny, but they laughed—because their navigation was good, because they had proved themselves once again to be masters of the vast sea, because safety was ahead.

Abiel returned to his cabin then, and at last he slept like a baby.

CHAPTER 10

*T*HE DAY OF ATONEMENT CAME. In his observance of it, Abiel would eat no food until the stars appeared on the following evening.* Ordinarily he would do no work either; but even the Pharisees agreed that a man could labor on the Holy Day if it was necessary to save life. Obviously, steering a ship fell into that category. So Abiel stood helm watch beneath the stars that night. The cloak he wore in the night's chill was his good, light-colored one, for it was customary to wear white on the Day of Atonement—a reminder, the rabbis said, of the words of Isaiah the Prophet: "Though your sins be as scarlet, they shall be as white as snow; though they be red like crimson, they shall be as wool."

Often as a child Abiel had heard those words in "Kol Nidre," the service held in the synagogue on the eve of the Fast. He had been puzzled, though, as to what they meant. What meaning indeed could they have for one like himself who had not sinned? As the stars made their long passage overhead, Abiel thought on these things. He thought on them alone, for Demaris did not come. Probably, he thought, she did not want to intrude on his observance of the Holy Day.

In the dim morning light, Crete loomed gray and misty out of the sea. In midmorning they rounded the eastern tip near Salmone and began beating westward once more against the

---

*The Jewish day was reckoned from sundown to sundown.

wind. But now, as Abiel had predicted, in the shelter of the island their westward progress was much faster.

Since the coast was only several stadia away, however, the centurion chained his prisoners in the passenger quarters so they would not be tempted to swim for freedom. Abiel was glad at least that he would see nothing of Paul during the days they worked up the coast.

He did, however, see a great deal of Demaris. She glowed with a spontaneous happiness whenever they met. *How beautiful she is*, Abiel would think as the breeze blew wisps of her light hair across her face—a face now upturned in confident cheer. Abiel enjoyed learning of her and perceived she was strong of spirit and wise in some ways, yet girlish and vulnerable in others. Since telling her of his plan, he was surprised at the strength of the attachment growing between them, a bond which made Ruth fade into dim memory. *Yes, how much better is Demaris for me*, Abiel thought, *than the cloistered Ruth would have been.*

At other times, though, Demaris withdrew into a tense, melancholy sadness. It was suspense, Abiel was sure. After all, to have freedom so tantalizingly in reach, yet to wonder constantly if the ship would indeed reach Puteoli in time to meet Phlegon's terms . . . Abiel too felt that gnawing fear, and both of them knew that Phlegon would not allow the slightest margin of grace.

Then, as they neared the Cretan city of Lasea, the shaft of the bilge pump broke, throwing both Coos and Plautus from the treadmill. Except for bruises, neither seaman was hurt, and Tychus, the ship's carpenter, soon had the pump working again. But the wooden drive shaft he used was the last one aboard. In spite of his intense desire to drive ever westward, Abiel knew they must stop at the nearest port to secure a new shaft; to be caught on the open sea with a broken bilge pump would mean disaster. So the next morning they sailed into the open harbor of Fair Havens near Lasea. Shipping from the little port had nearly ceased for the winter, and Abiel's huge ship coming across the breakwater caused a stir

in port. It was not often, even in summer, that a grain
freighter from Egypt put in at Fair Havens.

Calliades anchored a bit offshore among several smaller
ships. They let the boat down to ferry Tychus ashore, along
with anyone else who wanted to spend the night on land.
Farnaces took liberty to visit some relatives.

"Only one night here!" Abiel warned everyone. "We are
leaving first thing in the morning. We'll make the new shaft,
load some food, and be on our way!"

By mid-afternoon, Tychus had found a chandler to cut and
mill a new cypress shaft. Then both men rowed out to the ship
to match and drill the bolt key holes. There seemed no question
that everything would be ready for the continued trip west—
no question, that is, until Abiel was accosted on the deck by the
centurion. The Roman seemed agitated as he approached
Abiel, and his voice lowered confidentially. "Ben Heled, something has come up which I must tell you of. The prisoner Paul
has just told me a rather strange thing—strange, but I am inclined to take it seriously. He wants to meet with you and your
sailmaster as soon as possible."

"Spare me," said Abiel. "I'm of no mind to argue with him
over his Messiah!"

"No, no. Rather it has to do with the safety of your ship. It
could be urgent. Summon the sailmaster to your cabin; I and
Paul will join you there in a moment." Without waiting for any
further objections, Julius marched briskly down the compan-
ionway steps.

It was an irritable shipmaster who, with Calliades, met Roman and prisoner in his cabin. "What is this complaint about
the ship's safety?" Abiel snapped.

"I have no complaint," said Paul, "but a warning." Usually
the old apostle was pleasant and encouraging, but now his
face was grave as he sat beneath the flickering lamp. "Gentlemen," he said, "as you are aware, the Day of Atonement has
passed, and we are into the season when most shipmen consider it too dangerous to sail. And now, just this noon as I
communed in prayer with the Christ to whom I belong," he

looked up at Abiel, "I perceived that if we continue this voyage, it will be with great loss—not only of the cargo and ship, but our lives."

And then the cabin was silent as Paul's words simply lay there, untouched by anyone. Leaning against the bulkhead with arms folded, Abiel slowly ran a big hand across his bearded jaw. "*That* is what you wished to tell us?"

"Yes."

The shipmaster frowned as if at a poor joke. "There is no reason, Paul, for you or any of the other prisoners to be alarmed. We are aware of the weather this time of year, and we are observing it closely."

"I am not questioning your competence, Captain," said Paul. "I am telling you as directly as I know how—God has shown me that this ship will be wrecked if we continue this voyage."

At Paul's direct gaze, Abiel became uneasy. Did Paul *know* his plans to sail north again across the open sea to Greece? Did he know *why?* "Perhaps," Abiel said carefully, "you mean we might wreck if we were to leave the shelter of Crete?"

"No," said Paul. Then with each word he tapped the table with his finger. "I mean we will wreck *if we so much as leave this port.*"

In the shadows beneath the lamp, the centurion's face was dark and somber. "Paul, how do you *know* this? Is this one of the powers you spoke of, that the Nazarene has given you?"

"Yes," said Paul simply, "to attest the fact He *is* the Messiah and I am His apostle. I have direct communion at times through the Holy Spirit as did our prophets of old—thus the ability at times to know of future things."

"Well, will there be a storm to wreck us, or what?"

"I don't know. I don't know how it will happen. But I am earnestly warning all of you. If we leave this port, this ship is doomed."

At Paul's utter conviction, apprehension grew in the smoky cabin. Abiel could see it on Calliades' face; the sailmaster had been nervous lately anyway. The centurion's face was deeply troubled as well. Abiel began to pace slowly, still rubbing his jaw as he did when in deep thought. From whatever source it came, no captain could hear such a warning of doom and ignore it. Yet, to stay here would mean he would never win freedom for Demaris . . .

Then, quite suddenly, the utter foolishness of the situation hit Abiel, and he laughed out loud as he turned to the others. "Men, I think we see here a prisoner who wishes to delay his arrival in Rome as long as possible. And we see him making fools of us."

"Ben Heled, can you dismiss it so lightly?" asked the centurion.

"Has Paul convinced you that Jesus is God?"

The centurion paused. "No. No, he hasn't."

"Then there is no warning to heed, since Jesus is supposedly where it came from. There is no reason we should listen to a word Paul says."

"But, Ben Heled, neither have you convinced me the Nazarene is *not* your Messiah." Julius turned to Paul in exasperation. "Do you see my dilemma?"

"Yes." Paul nodded soberly. "The decision of who Jesus is— that is a decision all men must make. Usually it is not forced upon one so abruptly, though. Whatever you decide, I urge you to stay in this port."

"Very well," the centurion said softly. "Suppose we follow your advice and stay in port for the winter. We will be safe, and yet we will never know for sure if you were telling the truth, would we?" He looked quizzically at Paul. "We will never know what *would* have happened if we had left."

At the Roman's mention of spending the winter in Fair Havens, Abiel's jaw hardened and his voice came low with ill-concealed anger. "I have no intention of spending the winter here, this far from Rome."

"Are you forgetting," said Julius, "it is not your decision?"

"Are you forgetting you have no right to delay a commercial ship?"

"I certainly *do* have that right."

On snap inspiration, Abiel leveled a finger at the centurion. "Then you may be sure I will implead your government for my losses. And . . ."

"I have no doubt you will!" Julius cut in sharply. Then he looked up at the lamp as if imploring it for wisdom. "And then," he went on softly, "the legatus will ask me why I delayed the ship. And I will have to tell him I was frightened by the prediction of a Jewish religious teacher."

With that, Julius pounded his fist to the table and swore. "You Jews!" he snarled to Abiel and Paul both. "I still say, if you don't kill me, you will drive me insane!" Rising from the table, he strode to the door and jerked it open. "Gaius! Take Paul back to quarters, will you?"

As Paul followed the soldier out, he turned for a last look at the three. "My fellows, I've warned you. I've told you the sober truth. I've done all that I can do."

When he was gone, the tension seemed to lift slightly as with the cool air blowing through the open door. Seated back at the table, Julius glared at Abiel. "Ben Heled, *you* know your Scriptures, whereas I do not. And you know if there is any chance at all that Paul may be right!"

"That is true," said Abiel.

"Then what do you propose we do?"

"As I told you, I see no reason whatever to heed his warning."

"Are you willing to stake the lives of two hundred and seventy-six people on that?"

Abiel paused too long before he spoke. "Yes."

"Hmmph!" snorted the Roman. "I'm glad to see you have the confidence I lack. Because I know very well that Paul is not a madman. I don't know what he saw that day outside Damascus, but I do know *he* is sure of what he saw. And in spite of you, Ben Heled, I am inclined to heed his warning."

As usual, Abiel's anger steeled his mind and sharpened his wit; a possible solution came to him. "Then, if you really feel there is danger," he said curtly, "perhaps we can compromise."

"Compromise? With a warning like that?"

"Yes. You see, Fair Havens is a very poor place to spend the winter. Calliades will vouch for that."

As Abiel knew he would, the sailmaster stammered and hedged, unwilling to commit himself. "Well, this is a very exposed harbor," Calliades said finally. "If we remain here, we could take storm damage. Yes, I . . . I would not choose to winter here . . . ordinarily."

"We would be foolish to stay here," Abiel cut in, "especially when there is a very good and safe harbor just a day's voyage up the coast at Phoenix."

"That is your compromise?"

"Yes. We would sail close inshore," said Abiel, "in case any bad weather should arise, or any trouble develops with the ship. There would be no danger in a short trip like that, close in." Abiel stopped with that, not telling Julius the rest of his plans. Once they were safely at Phoenix, Paul would be proven the liar he was. And then Abiel would proceed on north to the Aegean, just as he had planned.

"Why don't you and I together examine the weather tomorrow morning?" Abiel went on. "We will leave here only if the weather is good, only if there is no danger."

The centurion drummed his fingers on the table for a moment. The growing relief on his face was obvious. This was just the sort of solution he needed—he could not be accused of yielding to a Jewish holy man, yet he would not be totally ignoring Paul's warning, either.

"It is your ship, Ben Heled," he said finally. "Any loss would be doubly yours." Abruptly he rose from the table. "Well, enough of this. May you sleep well tonight, gentlemen."

But that night they did not sleep well. The centurion tried a few drinks of wine, then forced himself to stop. He simply could not afford a swollen, fogged brain in the morning. Oh, yes, how convenient it would be, he thought, if tomorrow's dawn would bring foul weather. Then the decision would be made for him, and he could crawl back into bed and taste the wine.

That would be the coward's way out, perhaps. "But why not?" Julius mumbled to himself. Lately, in dealing with the Jews, he had become quite adept at taking the coward's way out.

Abiel, too, lay awake, with the centurion's challenge echoing in his brain. Was he really willing to gamble two hundred seventy-six lives on the fact that Jesus the Nazarene was a fraud? From long ago the words of Shemuel returned to haunt him: *If Jesus was not the Messiah, then who was He?* Groaning, Abiel tossed and pulled the woolen covers up. At the root of his problem, of course, was Demaris. Tentatively he asked himself if she was worth the risk.

As if in answer from the night there came a soft knock at the cabin door, and from the very softness of it Abiel had an inkling of who it might be. A gentle excitement welled within as he pulled on his tunic in the darkness, then opened the door. Dim in the darkness she stood, wearing the white cloak as she had on that first night she had come to talk with him. His pulse quickened. "Demaris?"

"Abiel, I'm sorry to awaken you," she said softly.

"I . . . I wasn't sleeping."

"Abiel, I *must* talk to you—and quickly, in case Lydas comes out on deck and sees us."

"In here?" Abiel swallowed.

"No, no. Let's walk on the deck," she murmured quickly. "If Phlegon does see us, it would appear we are only strolling, with nothing to hide."

Perplexed, Abiel walked with her to the rail amidships. Laughter was echoing across the water from a dockside tavern, and lights swam and shimmered on the dark, waxy sheen of the harbor. Leaning against the rail, he turned to see, in the dim reflected light, the corners of her lovely full lips compressed. Hers was the face of a child who had been told a disturbing fable. But even in her somber distress, Abiel found her charming. "Oh Demaris, my love," he breathed. "What is wrong?"

"Abiel," her voice trembled slightly, "I couldn't rest. I couldn't sleep because I heard what Paul has warned will happen to your ship."

"Demaris . . ."

"Abiel, I can't bear that you would lose your ship—even your life—because of me."

Gently Abiel put his finger across her lips. "Enough. Say no more of that." Sighing deeply, he looked out across the water.

Nearby loomed the other ships at anchor—dark silent hulks, lost and adrift in some dim nether world. They deepened the gloom. "Demaris," he sighed. "Paul sits down there, a common criminal, chained to other criminals like himself. We should all be laughing at him. Instead, the whole ship trembles at every word he says. What fools we are."

"Perhaps it is because he is *not* a common criminal, Abiel. There is nothing common about him at all."

"Neither is there anything truthful about him."

"Even so . . . there is still the danger." Her voice was flat and emotionless now. "Several days ago, when we crossed over to Crete, I heard your sailors curse you—out of your hearing. They knew the risk. I know you are taking risks for me." Her voice trembled anew. "But there are hundreds of other people on this ship, Abiel. And I cannot bear it."

"Demaris, enough of this. Listen to me: I *will* leave this harbor, if for no other reason than to prove that Paul and his Messiah both are utter liars. Nothing will keep me from that." Gently then he pulled her toward him. "And, my love, if I choose to take a risk because I love you, is it not my choice? You are not responsible."

"But I *am* responsible. That's why I had to see you tonight, Abiel, and tell you . . ." Her voice began trembling again. She took a deep breath. "I have to tell you I have lied to you. I have not been truthful . . ."

She leaned her head against his chest, and Abiel could feel her shake as she stifled the sobs. In his mind there welled a questioning void. "Demaris? What do you mean?"

After a moment she looked up and smoothed her hair back. "Oh Abiel, listen to me. Before you ever sailed your ship into Myra, Lydas knew he had to reach Rome with that money before winter. The moment he saw your ship, he concocted a plan. I was part of it. And so, from the first day I saw you from that sedan chair on the dock, I planned to trick you."

"Trick me?"

"Phlegon knows how to manipulate people. He understands a good man like you, and how to take advantage of you." Her voice lowered to a whisper. "And I am so sorry, Abiel."

A burning, leaden void gripped his chest and seemed to choke his breathing. "I can't accept this . . . can't believe it. You were in league with Phlegon? The first night you came to me on the aft deck, you were in league with Phlegon?"

"I had no choice." Her wet eyes reflected the shore lights. "I knew I was deceiving you. But after Paul's warning, I couldn't go on with it. I had to tell you."

Abiel tilted her head back slightly to look directly into her face for a moment. "If you have no love for me, why do you care? Why do you warn me and lose your chance for freedom?"

She was silent.

"Perhaps at first you didn't love me, or even intend to. But things have changed. Isn't it true you love me now?"

"Abiel, no matter what I answer, why should you believe a word I say?"

"Because you are risking your master's wrath to warn me, and you were crying a moment ago in my arms."

She stiffened then and became angry. "No, Abiel! I *don't* love you. Do you hear me? Not enough to see you endanger hundreds of people. No, not that much!"

Suddenly there came the scraping of sandals across the planks, and a dark form appeared from the shadows. They both looked up, startled to see Lydas Phlegon. "Well," he said. "What have we here? A little stroll in the night air?"

"It's good for the health," said Abiel.

"Nonsense. It's good for catching malaria. And speaking of health . . ." Phlegon seized Demaris roughly by the arm, "didn't I command you to stay below deck? You've disobeyed me."

"Be careful, Lydas," Abiel growled softly.

"No, *you* be careful, Captain. She is not yours yet, and we are much too close to land for her to be tempted with escape up here." He tugged her. "Come."

"Abiel, I'm sorry," she murmured. "Remember what I asked you."

"Don't be sorry." He stood seething and perplexed as they went into the dark. But after a few steps, Phlegon turned.

"Captain, I trust you will not be swayed by the rumors we are hearing—forecasts of doom from our imprisoned holy man."

Abiel paused a moment, wishing he could see Demaris' face in the dark. "No," he said finally. "You needn't worry. We sail from here in the morning."

"Good. I'm glad to see you are a man of your word."

Master and slave faded into the darkness. But once inside the lighted forward passageway, Phlegon pushed her savagely against the wall and grasped her wrist in an iron grip. "Now! What were you telling Ben Heled up there?"

Startled, she moaned and tried to pull away, as pain and anger filled her eyes.

"What were you telling him?"

"Nothing! We were talking about Paul. That's all."

"No, that is not all! Did you tell him about our plan?" He squeezed harder on her wrist. "You were trying to persuade him to stay here, weren't you!"

"Lydas," she threatened through clenched teeth, "I'll scream, and people will come out."

He released her, and she pulled away from him, sobbing softly.

"Let that be a lesson." Lydas was breathing hard. "I should think you would care about winning your freedom! Why are you so worried about Ben Heled?"

"Because . . . I don't want to see him hurt."

"You had best think of your own hurt. You know what the Romans do to slaves who disobey their masters! Why do you risk my anger?"

Her eyes flashed. "Because he is a *good* man, Lydas, and he loves me! I never knew what love was until I saw it in him." Her voice lowered. "And I love him more than I've ever thought I could love anyone. I had to tell him the truth. So go ahead with your anger. I *did* tell him!"

Her head snapped back as he struck her across the mouth. Phlegon drew his arm back to do it again. But the hatch door slammed open then, and it was Phlegon's turn to be frightened. At Abiel's menacing approach, the merchant reached into the folds of his vestment.

"Leave your dagger sheathed," Abiel growled, "Or I'll break your arm." Grabbing the merchant by the tunic with one huge hand, Abiel slammed him back against the wall. Phlegon's turban went flying, and greasy, foul hair fell across the slave trader's forehead. Abiel thrust him back, thumping his bare head against the wall again, and held him there, pinned at the neck.

"Ben Heled!" Phlegon squeaked, his eyes bulging in terror, "you're mad!"

"Be sure of it," Abiel hissed. "Never again. Understand me. You will never abuse her again."

"Yes. Yes, of course!" Lydas quavered. "I promise you."

Abruptly, Abiel released the merchant, who sagged against the wall, trembling and coughing. Several wide-eyed passengers, jarred from sleep, came out into the passageway. Abiel ignored them as he turned to Demaris. "You're bleeding," he murmured.

"Yes." With a trembling hand the girl dabbed at the trickle of blood at her mouth. "It will be all right. Thank God you came, Abiel."

"Before I came in, I was listening. I heard what you told Phlegon."

She looked up, dismay and longing mixed in her eyes. "I wish you hadn't heard, Abiel." She began to cry. "But I'm glad you know. I do love you."

Abiel motioned to the spectators. "Back inside." Then he took her in his arms and whispered, "Demaris, if I had to sail this ship into Hades for you, I'd do it."

CHAPTER 11

AT DAWN ABIEL WAS ON THE AFT DECK. Silhouetted like a statue against the eastern glow, he watched the sunrise and smelled the air. The cook, making his way to the galley, saw him there and knew why the captain watched so closely the dawning of this day. Everyone who had remained aboard *Athelia* overnight knew what Paul had warned, an amazing thing since Paul himself had told no one and would answer no questions about his strange meeting with the ship's officers.

As the sun rose gleaming over the harbor landhead, the centurion climbed to the aft deck. Wearing his heavy winter cloak, he exchanged gruff greetings with Abiel.

"There is no redness in the sunrise," Abiel said.

The centurion cursed inwardly; his hopes for an easy way out were not going to be realized. Carefully he scanned the horizon, where not a cloud could be seen. Fate, it seemed, had closed him in. He looked positively pale.

Abiel, wary of his silence, did not want to urge him too hard. "Would you care for an early breakfast?"

"No." Julius sighed and leaned against the rail, looking outward. Then he paced for a few minutes, and as he did so there came a barely perceptible stirring of the air. Small ripples on the water heralded its presence; in the swath of the rising sun they sparkled like a thousand diamonds.

"This breeze should grow," said Abiel. "It's a breeze from the south—exactly what we need."

"Well, the day does look good. Some of our passengers are

very nervous over this. Oh yes. The news has gotten out; don't ask me how."

"Perhaps if we told our nervous ones this will be only a short trip . . . We won't even hoist the boat aboard; we will just tow it behind us. That should make them feel better."

"Well, I suppose we really should go. There is no reason we should not." At Abiel's obvious relief, the centurion scowled. "So now, Ben Heled, at last we will find out who is telling the truth, won't we? You or Paul? Has that thought occurred to you?"

"Of course it has," said Abiel.

And so Calliades, himself strangely subdued, signaled the harbor master by heliograph that *Athelia* would weigh anchor soon. Shortly afterward, a gong sounded over the harbor, alerting passengers and crew alike.

Hurrying Pasher through his breakfast, Abiel detailed him and several others to row ashore for as many of the crew as they could handle. The others would have to ferry out with local boatmen. The men rowed ashore quite slowly, it seemed, and Abiel could easily hear their voices murmuring over the water, discussing the rumors of disaster. They did not want to leave Fair Havens.

It was nearly the second hour of day before everyone was back aboard—everyone, that is, except Farnaces. As Abiel paced the deck, his first mate appeared waving at the docks. A local boat boy rowed him out to the ship and, after the usual haggling and shouting over the fare, a grinning Farnaces was soon up the gang ladder with his sea bag.

"We were about to leave without you," said Abiel. "Come on. Let's get them moving."

"Are we heading up the coast, sir?"

"To Phoenix—today at least."

As they got the ship underway, Farnaces soon found himself growing irritated indeed. The men at the anchor lines acted as if they were sleepwalking. The topsail handlers climbed the mast with great gloom and lethargy, as if going to their doom, and the forward crew had the foresail luffing and flapping like a group of amateurs.

"Come on, look alive! Move it!" Farnaces roared. "By the gods, what's wrong with you people this morning?" He was indeed baffled, for the morning was beautiful. The autumn sky was burning blue, so that the water appeared almost black against it. Back on the aft deck with Abiel and Calliades, he commented on the strange lack of enthusiasm. "They act like they're under a spell, sir."

"If you must know, they are," said Abiel.

"What?"

"It's the Christian, Paul," grinned Calliades at the rudders. "He has predicted our ship will go down if we leave this harbor. We are all going to drown. Nothing serious."

"Are you jesting?"

"No." Abiel growled. "He isn't. Paul warned of something like that. Just so you know. It has everyone nervous."

"Well," Farnaces shrugged. "Just so the men do their jobs."

The whole situation was becoming insane, Abiel thought. A few minutes later, as he stood scowling at the rail, he thought of a way to improve it. "Look," he told Calliades, "we have to get some life in this ship. Steer toward the tanner's house there until you come even with the docks. Then head her out. Farnaces, have the men keep those sails trim."

Calliades nodded and understood. In steering that course, they would leave the harbor with the wind on the aft quarter. In that configuration, the *Athelia* was at her best.

True to herself, the ship picked up quickly. She pulsed and sang, and they lowered the yard to trim her better. The skipper was right, Calliades thought. How could anybody worry when the ship was like this? Yes, if they were going to embark on a fatal voyage, they would at least do it in style—boiling out of the harbor, leaving a wake, throwing a sheet of spray from the bow.

On a rise of land near the harbor entrance was an elegant inn and tavern, a retreat for wayfaring patricians and the wealthy of Lasea. The dining room emptied as the elegant ones streamed out to view the brave ship thundering by so close, flecks of foam sweeping past her sides and a rainbow glistening in her bow spray. They cheered and waved, and calls of "Where to?" echoed over the water.

"To Phoenix! To Phoenix today!" The passengers shouted and waved back from the railing.

Abiel watched the display for a while and grinned at Calliades. "We have here a definite improvement in morale."

Through the rest of that beautiful morning they sailed west. With the wind steadily aft of the port beam, the men on duty had an easy time. After sweeping down the decks, they lounged in the sun along with the passengers and soon began to enjoy this remarkable autumn day. How timid their fears seemed, indeed, out in the brightness, while Paul and his warnings remained locked away in the passengers' quarters.

To keep everyone at ease, Abiel ordered Calliades to steer as close inshore as was prudent. The ship's boat they simply towed behind them. After the uneventful passage of an hour or more, the shipmaster's heart exulted. So much for Paul and his absurd warnings. So much for his Nazarene Messiah!

It was with a happy confidence that Abiel talked with Demaris at the bow rail. In the sunlight she, too, was much less fearful than the evening before. She joked wryly about her swollen lip, and Abiel laughed even at that. Yes, he had not realized just how heavy was the burden on him, lifted now from his heart and buoyed skyward by the brilliance of sunlight. "Did I not tell you Paul was a liar?" he smiled. Then his voice softened so no one else could hear. "We will press on thus. And we will soon have your freedom."

He took his noon meal in his cabin. Then, because the last two nights had been mostly sleepless, he lay his head on folded arms for a brief rest. Without meaning to, he fell asleep.

The ship fell away, and he stood in a dream at the foot of a barren desert hill. Looking upward, he blinked and sheltered his eyes, and he saw a cross silhouetted against the sun. At the top of it were the words, THIS IS THE KING OF THE JEWS. But the cross was empty, and as Abiel stared at it, the sun went black and he felt the earth shift beneath his feet. He cried out in terror—then awoke with a start to find himself back in the familiar surroundings of his cabin.

But something had changed. It was not the earth that had shifted, but his ship. The *Athelia* was leaning to port—which meant the wind must have changed very suddenly while he had slept. And then the porthole darkened as the sun disappeared behind a cloud. It was with a vague, rising dread that Abiel opened the cabin door, to be met immediately by a very apprehensive Farnaces. "I was just coming to get you, sir." The first mate gestured toward the north. "That has been coming up pretty fast."

To the north, over the rocky hills and ravines of Crete, rose a solid bank of dark stratus clouds, filling the sky like a grayish-black liquid. Jagged pieces of cloud ran far ahead of the mass, and though the surface wind was moderate, Abiel's stomach tightened to see the alarming speed with which the wind was driving the clouds. The sun came out again, this time weak and pale with an ominous, cold light. Abiel's jaw went slack. "Perhaps . . . perhaps we should get some men aloft and furl the topsails," he told Farnaces. "Just as a precaution, you understand." Then, trying to appear at ease, he ignored the faces of crew and passengers and made his way to the aft deck stairs, making a point to climb them slowly.

Calliades was greatly relieved to see him. "What do you think of *that*, sir?"

Abiel turned to study the clouds again. "Perhaps a little squall," he lied. "A little rain."

"Well, to me it looks like a *big* squall. I say we had best put into that little inlet over there. We should get in as close as we can and anchor. We could move in slow and sound the depth as we go."

Abiel rubbed his jaw. "Too risky," he said. "There are rocks all along there, and if we don't detect one, we'll tear the bottom out." He took a deep breath. "If the weather *really* starts to get bad, we'll find a better place ahead."

"Sir . . ." Calliades' voice was a pleading quaver. "You heard what Paul said yesterday . . ."

"Has Paul turned you all into sheep?" snapped Abiel.

"And has Paul made you a lunatic?" Calliades shot back, jabbing his finger to the north. "Can't you see what's coming up over there?"

Abiel bit his lip. The clouds had become personal things. In them was the dark shadow of the Nazarene, the shadow that had haunted him for years. *The Nazarene lives!* the clouds rumbled. *And you have played the fool.*

Abiel's back stiffened. "You have your orders," he turned to Calliades. "Keep her moving as she is. If you don't, I will."

The centurion was there suddenly, having come quickly up the aft deck stairs. He strode to the captain. "Should we anchor there, Ben Heled?" he asked crisply. "Your men say over there is a possible place. What Paul warned is coming to pass."

"We've discussed that inlet," said Abiel coldly. "Will Paul guarantee there are no submerged boulders over there, so we won't puncture the hull and sink?"

"Well, where *can* we put in?"

"At Phoenix!" snapped Abiel. "Haven't you seen clouds and rain before? This ship can float in the rain!"

At that moment the wind rose perceptibly, heeling the ship more. Julius grasped the rail and glared at Abiel as, below on the main deck, the crew scrambled to slacken sheets.

"Ben Heled," Julius hissed, "our blood will be on you."

"Since when does a Roman worry about blood?" said Abiel. "Certainly not in Caesarea!"

Julius cursed him. "You and your deceit!" he spat. "What was the use of our staying close to shore if we can't put in?"

"We will find a more suitable place ahead if the weather should really warrant it."

"Do you *know* if there is a better place?"

"No."

Julius swore again. Obviously unsure of what he should do, he went to the rail to study the sky again.

With the fresher wind they were moving along the coast faster, making good speed indeed. But with each moment the promising inlet fell further astern, and the centurion along with the crew began straining their eyes for a better haven ahead. Tension aboard the ship was stifling.

As the dark mass moved higher, a knot in Abiel's stomach drew tighter. He had hoped and prayed that a clearing would soon show beneath the rising clouds, that there would be only a rain squall and nothing more. But the clearing did not appear. Finally the clouds rose high enough to blot out the sun, and in the darkening gloom the crew and passengers stared at one another, white-faced.

They heard it coming from across the land—the roar of wind and rain. Ripples of driven water marked its pitiless approach. Abiel could not meet his sailmaster's eye. The sudden gust roared into the ship, heeling them hard to port. Several passengers fell. A woman screamed. Calliades instinctively steered into the wind, trying to bring the mainsail oblique to it so the ship could straighten. But the wind was so strong that the ship could not turn into it. "By Cybele!" Calliades gasped.

Immediately Abiel and Farnaces began shouting orders to square the mainsail so the ship could come back level. Seamen rushed to obey, screaming at the awe-stricken passengers to get out of the way. As they hauled on the starboard brace, a corner of the mainsail tore loose and began to flap and crack like thunder. The brail lines flew askew, writhing in the wind, and the vibration of it drummed through the deck. Only seconds remained, Calliades knew, before the sail shredded and blew away. Worse, if a second brace tore loose, the sail could swing square to the wind, and the ship would capsize for sure. So, without waiting for orders—while he still had some forward speed—he leaned to his rudders and pointed *Athelia* away from the wind. Quickly she swung, and, to the relief of all, she slowly came back level again. Level—but blowing out to sea away from land and any safety they may have found.

As the crew wrestled the sail under control again, shortening it to stabilize the ship, a stinging deluge of rain blew into them. A few soaked and frightened passengers began making their way to the hatch, while others huddled and craned their necks to see the fading land. Abiel saw Demaris among them, looking up at him. He pretended not to see her.

He did not reprimand Calliades, for the sailmaster had done what was needed to save the situation; but uppermost in his mind now was the thought that they must not blow out to sea. "Do you think," he shouted to Calliades, "we could rig a lateen and tack back toward the coast?"

"In this wind? Are you crazy?" Rain streamed down the sailmaster's face, and his eyes blazed in accusation. "You had your chance back when we passed up that inlet! You can forget it now until this wind dies—which it won't!"

Abiel looked stricken as he saw the coast of Crete had already disappeared behind them in the gloom and driving rain. Paul's warning was coming true. A suffocating sensation rose in Abiel's breast, and he swallowed hard to push it back down, like a snake into its basket. He could not afford to panic. He must forget Paul, and all else, and concentrate only on saving the ship.

Farnaces scrambled back on the aft deck. "Sir, at this rate we'll blow to Africa. Let me have them strike sail and put out the sea anchor!"

"No!" Abiel's voice was quivering, and he fought to control it, shouting above the wind. "The island, Cauda, is out there ahead somewhere. We will need the sail to steer around it. Get two lookouts at the bow and tell them to listen for shoals!"

Farnaces paled and hurried away.

And so the ship drove under shortened sail before the wind. Under Calliades' control, she was stable and plowing through waves which had not yet begun to mount over six feet. But all hope of safety was gone in the rain behind them.

Everyone seemed suddenly aware of the cold. The crew began going below for their oiled mantles and leggings. And the passengers simply huddled together, wondering what would happen in the dark hours ahead.

"People, listen to me." In the smoky glow of the suspended lamps, Abiel's hollow voice echoed through the cabin where the passengers sat in miserable, wet suspense. Facing them was the hardest thing he had ever done, and he looked past them all to speak directly to the one he wanted so badly to trust him, Demaris. "We are running out to sea before this wind," he went on, "and the ship is stable. There is no danger in this." He tried to smile at her. "Tomorrow, after this storm blows itself out, we will only have to sail back the way we came. It is that simple."

There were immediate rising murmurs of disbelief. "Didn't Paul say this ship was going to sink?" A woman's voice rang out, high and harsh. "Paul, didn't you warn all of them before we left Fair Havens? Didn't you?"

A sudden roar of voices drowned Abiel's further words, but the passengers seemed to be arguing with each other as much as directing any malice toward the captain. It was then that Paul, the sturdy little man with the chains, stood up and motioned for silence. Nothing could have quieted the room faster, and suddenly the roar of wind and rain could be heard again. Abiel was surprised when Paul looked to him respectfully. "Captain," he said loudly, "may I have your permission to speak?"

Trapped, Abiel could only nod his agreement.

"Thank you." Paul's voice carried easily throughout the cabin. "My fellows, the captain has told you the truth. We are driving well, and there is no danger."

Shouts and questions arose. "Will the storm blow out? What was your warning? Tell us!"

Again Paul motioned for silence. "It is true I went to the captain's cabin yesterday to discuss the dangers of sailing this late in the year. There are many rumors as to what was said there. I, for one, will not even discuss them because it is pointless now to do so. Our captain and this ship have been through storms worse than this, I would suppose. He knows what he is doing. Listen to what he says."

Paul then went back to Lucanus and his own group, as relaxed as if in the safest room ashore. The murmurs rose again. Plainly the passengers were not satisfied at what they had heard, but Paul's confidence comforted them more than his words. Abiel could only look at Paul in some wonder. The "apostle" had been given a perfect opportunity to embarrass him, yet had not done so. Abiel nodded his silent thanks.

Leaving the passenger cabin, he was surprised to see that Demaris had slipped out of the women's side and was waiting for him in the passageway. "Demaris . . ." he murmured.

"Oh, Abiel, what have we done?"

"You have done nothing, nor have I. Tomorrow you will see." Not caring if anyone saw, he drew her to him, and she felt his trembling.

Not long afterward that evening, the lookouts reported breakers in the distance. Waves were booming ashore in the rocky hollows and crevices of what must be the island of Cauda. Abiel ordered immediate soundings of the water depth, while the crew strained their eyes peering through the driving mist of twilight. But the sounding leads never struck bottom, and they never caught sight of the island. When Calliades deemed they were safely past Cauda, he steered east slightly, thinking that the wind might abate some if they could get in the lee of the island. Then he advised Abiel to get the ship's boat aboard while they still had the chance—the captain had forgotten about it entirely.

It was a fiendishly hard job in the murky light to wrestle the plunging boat alongside the ship toward the davits, while other seamen held it away from the hull with staving poles. But the shivering men worked willingly, knowing the boat might be the only salvation for a lucky few if the ship should run aground.

Then, because Paul's somber gaze of warning was now etched in his mind, Abiel held a tense conference with Calliades and Farnaces and then ordered his tired crew to a task he had hoped to avoid. They began hauling out the hull-banding cable.

The ship's hull, beneath the copper sheets below the waterline, was constructed of planks joined together with mortise-and-tenon joints. It was stout and well made, but if the hull frame ever buckled or twisted, cracks could open between the planks. Thus, like most ships of her day, *Athelia* carried lengths of esparto cable that could be worked back underneath the hull and, at intervals, lapped over the deck and fastened to strengthen the whole assembly. Whether these bands really did any good or not was a subject of much debate among shipmen. Those who had used them in storms swore by their effectiveness. Of course, captains who had seen them fail were generally not around to tell about it.

Abiel had hesitated to order the job done, knowing such an order would be an admission that the ship was in trouble. Even now he assured the crew that they were doing it now only because it would be easier to work the rope back along the hull while the ship was still moving forward under sail. "Only a precaution," he insisted. And he hoped the crew, whether they believed it or not, would at least pass that word along to the passengers.

The last two cable loops were run and fastened in roaring wet darkness. Only light from the hatchways and the open shutters of Abiel's cabin illuminated the blowing rain and gave the staggering, exhausted seamen any reference of direction.

Then, in the darkness, they struck sail completely, brailling up the mainsail tightly to the yardarm. Somewhere to the south, they knew, lay the quicksands and shallows of the African coast. So, from the bow, they let down the sea anchor, a conical frame covered with slotted leather skin which, by offering resistance to the water, slowed the ship's drift and held the bow toward the wind and waves.

Amid the feverish work, the cook managed his usual evening meal, along with his wonderful hot drink of herbs and honey. The huddled passengers, as they half-heartedly ate, remarked how strange it seemed to remember that only a few hours ago they had been sailing easily under sunny skies.

At last, when Coos lit the lamp in Abiel's cabin that night, the dripping, disheveled shipmaster found himself confronted by the centurion, who having followed the seaman in, emerged with the light like some mischievous god in a Greek drama.

"Well," growled Abiel. "The day is full of surprises."

"Unfortunately," said the Roman. "Well, Captain, that was quite a performance you gave today in the passenger cabin. Do you really believe it?"

"Believe what?"

"That the storm will be over by tomorrow! Or is it more likely we are finding out Paul was telling the truth?"

Wet clothes and all, Abiel sank onto his pallet. In the lamplight his face was blank with weariness. "Don't you see I cannot afford to give up?" he said softly. "If Paul is right, do you realize what it means for all of us?"

The centurion swallowed. "Perhaps . . . perhaps if we plead with Paul, he would spare us."

"Do you think he is God," flared Abiel, "that he can command a storm?"

"It is very obvious now he speaks from God!"

"Nothing of the sort. You were there. Paul did not forecast a storm; he said he didn't know *how* it would happen! This . . . this could only be coincidence, and it could be over tomorrow."

"I think we know very well it will not be, Ben Heled. And I think we know now who was telling the truth. So now . . . you Jews and your God have finally killed me, haven't you?" Julius cursed bitterly. "I suppose now I must decide what to do with this 'truth' before I die of it."

CHAPTER 12

*T*HAT NIGHT Calliades, Pasher, and his men took the watch. But there was little they could do except take occasional soundings and check the banding cables, the hatches, the bilge, and the sea anchor. They spent most of their time trying to keep warm in the galley. The captain was up every hour checking the weather. With face pale, he would stand with Calliades beside the firepit. "This should be over by morning," he kept repeating. "It should blow over by noon at the latest, don't you think?"

There was something ridiculous in the question. Here it was in late autumn. The wind howled outside, drumming against the ship like a wagon rolling over a hollow culvert. The exploding rain hissed and blew like sand—and here was the captain saying it would soon be over, like a summer storm. Calliades would coldly agree. "Perhaps . . . I hope you are right." But both men sensed that the captain would not be right.

The seas began to mount. By the second watch of night, *Athelia* was beginning to slowly rise and plunge in the waves, and with each gyration Abiel's soul would wither more. By the third watch, the seas were high enough that Abiel knew he must put someone at the helm to keep the ship head on to the waves. To his relief, he found that Calliades was already there. Good old Calliades.

Finally, in the early hours before morning, unable to bear the growing agony in his soul, the sleepless captain went up to the aft deck himself. Twice he almost fell as the wind tried to topple him and the ship lurched. Barely visible in the darkness was the dark, wet hulk of Calliades who, when Abiel tapped his arm, jumped as if seeing a spirit from the deep. "Captain!"

"You better get below and warm up some," shouted Abiel. "I'll relieve you."

"You'll get your chance at this come daylight, Skipper," Calliades bawled. "What's your hurry?"

"The storm will be over by tomorrow evening. Why knock yourself out?"

A sickening plunge and shock made Calliades gasp involuntarily as the ship hit the bottom of a trough. "This won't be over any time soon, Abiel. You know that."

"All right! Perhaps it won't. But you go below. That's an order. And let me be alone up here for a while."

Calliades understood then. Sometimes wind and rain in the face can be a balm when it drowns the harsher pain within.

Soon Abiel was alone in the dark, roaring world. Cold rain came in sporadic bursts against his face while the wind tore back the hood of his cloak again and again. For a while he was glad for the punishment and the concentration it required of him, for it helped drive all other thoughts from mind. With the sea anchor slowing their backward drive, the rushing seas provided enough rudder effect that the helmsman could keep the bow pointed into the waves. In darkness it must be done by feel alone. Using the forward hatch lamp as a reference, Abiel steered toward whichever quarter rose into the wave first. The foaming crest would sweep past below him, hissing like a thousand snakes in the darkness. Then the ship would tilt and plunge, and with each cycle Abiel was forced to acknowledge that the waves were growing ever higher. He was glad to be alone.

Time lost all meaning and continuity. He knew morning had come only because their world turned from black to a forbidding gray. Now, able to see their danger, he almost wished it were still dark. Their world had contracted into a murky bowl. Into it the seas would swell and rise, toss the ship, and, as if fleeing the scene of their crime, roll aft to disappear into the driving mist. The whitecaps mounted only to be blown flat by the wind, and the flying foam stung like sand.

When Farnaces came to relieve his captain, he recoiled at the apparition before him. Salt had condensed and caked on Abiel's beard and mustache, and his red-rimmed eyes stared out like a madman's.

"By Zeus, you look awful!" the first mate shouted. "You had better get some rest, sir."

"No. I'd better check the ship."

"I already have! She's as tight as a rivet. I have men watching the sea anchor and keeping the bands tight. The bilge is fine; I've got two men on the pump."

"Do you have the spare belt and shaft ready?"

"Yes! And we're taking soundings every quarter-hour."

"Is that Marius on lookout?"

"Yes. He's fine. Now you'd better get below. The ship is fine."

"Well, I'll rest just for a moment." Abiel's last two nights had been sleepless, and this night had ended with five punishing hours at the helm. Staggering into his cabin, he collapsed on the pallet. The wind and rain had done their work. Whether Paul was right or not was immaterial now. Drained of all thought and emotion, he fell into an exhausted sleep.

In the few hours that Abiel slept, the waves grew higher still. The seamen, even in their fear, found a growing thankful amazement at the way their ship weathered the storm. The *Athelia* remained rock-steady as she pitched headlong into the dark, smooth hollows. She climbed like a sea bird into the towering green mountains of water. And each time, the sailors would pat her deck or rail in affectionate gratitude. Other ships, they knew, broke apart and died in seas like this.

About midmorning though, the *Athelia* did not climb fast enough to clear the top of one huge wave, and for the first time tons of water came crashing down on her deck. The crewmen saw it coming, but the soldier, Lupus, would have been lost had he not clung with arms and legs to a banding cable. He lost only his shoes and cape in the torrent that thundered across the deck, sweeping buckets, rope, and gear overboard.

The gangway flipped up, cracked against the rail, and swirled away aft.

A horrified Farnaces watched from the aft deck as, for a few heart-stopping seconds, the ship rolled from side to side as if in pain, spilling the water from her decks. Then, to everyone's relief, she began to climb again.

But then pandemonium broke out on deck as the off-duty crew and many passengers came boiling out of the forward hatchway, preferring to drown in the open. Abiel, jarred into heart-pounding wakefulness, bolted from his cabin and nearly ran into the ashen-faced centurion.

"What happened, Ben Heled?" the Roman rasped.

"I think we took a wave over the bow!"

"What can we do?"

"You can get out of my way!" Abiel snapped. The Roman seemed uncomprehending. Abiel, smelling the wine on his breath, left him in his bewilderment as he ran off to find Calliades and check the ship for damage.

The centurion then spied his wet, bedraggled, and aghast soldier.

"A wave . . . water, sir!" said Lupus. "It came over the ship!"

"*Over* the ship?" The centurion staggered slightly with another pitch of the deck.

"Yes, sir. I thought surely I was dead. Sir, you should get back inside. You're in no shape to be out here."

"Ship . . . a ship can't survive that!" Julius looked gravely at Lupus, rain and blowing mist streaming down his florid face. "Paul was right! Paul—not Ben Heled!"

"Sir, please go back inside!"

"Lupus, no matter what I tell you . . . don't bring me any more wine. That is an order."

"Yes, sir."

Back in Calliades' cabin, the centurion groaned. Paul was right. And, if he had at last found the bearer of truth, it seemed something should be done about it. Yes, the centurion thought. As soon as his mind cleared. As soon as his stomach stopped its rebellion, something should be done.

Though dreading to do so, Abiel rushed into the passenger cabin to check the bow struts. The area reeked of vomit, and he could not bear their haggard faces. If he had known how terrible he looked himself, he would have been ashamed for them to see him. But it seemed the *Athelia* was becoming a ship of madmen anyway—men with faces drawn and eyes red. It was no use, of course, trying to reassure anyone. Not after this.

Hurrying back out on deck, the captain was met by Farnaces. "Sir, it almost happened again! Another wave almost came over. Sir, we have to lighten the ship!"

"Lighten it?"

"Throw out the grain! The wine jars!"

Abiel's jaw shot out. With the sea as it was, he now knew he could be defeated. He could lose it all. Cornered, he fought back. "No!" he shouted over the wind. "This storm will die out by tomorrow. And then what? We go to Rome without a cargo. Who is going to pay your wages?"

"Wages!" Farnaces exploded. "We want our lives!"

"We keep the cargo!" shouted Abiel, and walked on toward the aft deck. Farnaces, joined by several frightened seamen, followed after him shouting and imploring, as if Abiel were the pied piper in a wind-ravaged asylum. Finally at the aft deck steps, Abiel paused and turned. "There is no need to jettison the cargo! Don't panic. Tomorrow you will be glad we kept it!"

"This storm isn't going to stop tomorrow," screamed Farnaces above the wind. "Sir, that Jewish teacher was right! Let's at least give the ship a fighting chance!"

From the dark anger on the captain's face then, Farnaces knew he had said the wrong thing. Abiel turned and went up the steps, gritting his teeth at the wind. "Paul is *not* right," he ranted. *"He cannot be right!"*

For a while they endured the pitch and sodden plunges of the ship. But later that afternoon, as Abiel and Calliades watched helplessly from the aft deck, another sea crashed down over the starboard quarter. Farnaces and Marius, the only crewmen on the main deck at that time, desperately clung—one to a cable, another to a stanchion. Cursing the sea and their captain, they held their breath as the water roared over them. This time the *Athelia* rose more slowly, wallowing sluggishly as water spilled from her railings. And the next coming wave simply rolled over the bow. As if in the slow motion of a dream, Abiel and Calliades watched it roll lazily aft, burying the entire front of the ship under a foaming mantle.

"She's going!" Calliades gasped.

Abiel prayed instinctively. "O Master of the Universe, no!" He would see Farnaces and Marius drown before his eyes!

At that moment something broke deep in Abiel's soul. Like the water rushing across his ship, the realization burst upon him that he had brought nearly three hundred people to their deaths. They would drown like rats in the hold down there—Demaris, all of them.

But miraculously the ship began to rise again, slowly, as the two men held their breath. "Come on! Come on, old girl!" Calliades urged, rising on tiptoe as if to take his own weight off her. As if in obedience, the *Athelia* wallowed through a smooth trough, rode over the next small wave, and by the time the next towering sea hit her was free of her burden. This time she rode defiantly over the wave.

Drenched and sputtering, Farnaces was coming angrily to the aft deck. But Calliades did not wait for him as, turning on Abiel, his curses enveloped the shipmaster like a typhoon. "*Now* will you lighten her?" he roared. "One more wave would have finished us!" He cursed again. "Do you want to see us die? You and your ambition! Isn't there something in your pious Jewish laws about murder?"

"Stop it!" Abiel snapped.

"No! Because that's what it is. Murder! I've watched you risk this ship, sailing across to Crete this time of year! You were even going to sail *back* north!"

Abiel grimaced then as if struck physically, as the vision of two hundred seventy-six drowned bodies flashed before his eyes. He almost fell as the ship plunged again. "Farnaces, get started with lightening the ship," he said. "Hurry! Use the passengers to help. Get everybody . . . get rid of the stuff. Just leave enough weight for ballast."

They stared at him for a moment in vindictive surprise. Then Farnaces hurried to begin the task, hoping it wasn't too late.

Abiel went to his cabin and sat a moment, his head buried in his hands. A little later, he helped them jettison the cargo. It disquieted the crew to see their captain pale, as if he had seen a ghost in the dark sky. He said little, and he left the details and supervision of the work to Farnaces.

Julius unchained his prisoners entirely so they could help. Farnaces formed a line of men from the cargo hold, up through mid-deck, to the large cargo hatch, to the main deck, and from there to the rail. Soon the sacks of grain, each half the weight of a man, were splashing over the side. Calliades, watching from the aft deck, smiled sadly. "No need to press on to Rome now, is there?" he muttered.

The passengers seemed glad to have something to do, to at least have a hand in their fate—however futile. They worked feverishly passing the bags, occasionally stumbling with a lurch of the ship. Twice waves broke on the deck and water coursed down on the terrified carriers. Still they worked, mechanically, woodenly. When one fell out from exhaustion, another would take his place. On into the night they worked— and saw their labors rewarded as the ship began to take on a greater buoyancy. Even the landlubbers could feel the fresh way she climbed the waves, the lighter shock when she hit the troughs.

As Abiel took his turn at the helm that night, it was with a flicker of hope. They may yet live—all of them. The sacrifice of his cargo had surely been a sacrifice to God, just as surely as if he had given a lamb to be placed on the altar in Jerusalem. "O Master of the Universe," he prayed to his faraway God, "reward me by letting us live. Reward me by yet proving Paul to be wrong."

Time began playing tricks on them all. In Calliades' cabin, Julius the centurion had no idea what hour of the night lay on them, when he sent for the prisoner Paul. He did so with much trepidation. Sober now, he knew very well he had been playing a game of sorts. All during the voyage he had practically dared both Paul and Ben Heled to show him the truth. Now there was something terrifying in the realization that he had found it.

Paul was wet when he arrived with Gaius at Calliades' cabin. He had been asleep, exhausted from passing the sacks of grain, yet as always he was gentle and gracious.

Julius' apology seemed genuine as he explained why he had sent for the apostle. "Paul, I've told you how I want to know who your God is. And now it seems I know who was telling the truth."

"Yes," said Paul.

"And now I want to know if there is a statue or likeness of Jesus the Messiah. You see, I have a statue of Augustus at a shrine in my villa in Ravenna. It is my most prized possession. But if your God will let us live, I will place a likeness of Jesus beside my emperor, and I will worship Jesus as well. I promise I will do that." The Roman looked at Paul hopefully.

"Oh Julius," Paul said wearily as to a child, "have you still not seen? Jesus is the conqueror of death—the God of all creation. When He soon returns to reign, every knee will bow to Him and every tongue confess that He is Lord! Julius, He cannot be confined to a mere image. And to place Him on the same level as Augustus would be the grossest denial of who He is."

The centurion swallowed, disappointed. "Paul! Please don't say I must place Him above my emperor."

"He is Lord of all," said Paul simply. "The only acceptable worship is to acknowledge Him as such."

"Paul, I cannot *do* that! You are a Roman. You know the oath I took as a soldier."

"Ah," Paul nodded. "The oath." Yes, he knew very well the words Julius had sworn: "I swear by the majesty of the emperor, who is to be loved and worshiped by the human race, that I will perform with enthusiasm whatever the emperor commands . . . that I will not shrink from death in my obedience . . ." It was an oath which captured the mind, soul, and body. Paul knew that a soldier like Julius would die before he violated it. He was silent a moment before speaking. "Julius, do you believe that Jesus, the Christos, is Lord of all?" he asked gently.

"What I have seen here proves it may be so," Julius said.

"Then," said Paul, "that means He is also the Lord of your emperor. So, do you see, if you accept your emperor's Lord as your own, you will be within the chain of command. You will not be violating your oath."

There was a flicker of hope, a raising of the head. Then the centurion's eyes narrowed in sudden irritation. "This wretched, plunging ship! It's not the place for rational thought! Do you expect me to desert my emperor because I am afraid I will die? Do you think I am afraid of the Jewish Messiah?"

"You will not be deserting your emperor . . . "

Before Paul could reply further, Julius snapped an order to the optio standing by. "Gaius, take Paul back to his quarters, please. Now."

The optio came to attention. "And is there anything else you require, sir?"

Julius thought a moment, then swore softly. "If . . . if there is any to be had, you may bring me a fresh skin of wine."

CHAPTER 13

*T*HE SHIPMASTER had no idea of how long he was at the helm that night. Nor did he know how long, in exhaustion, he slept the next morning. But he awoke sometime during the day to feel the most incredible fall he had ever known on a ship. It seemed the *Athelia* would plunge forever. When she finally struck the trough with a wrenching shock, Abiel knew the sacrifice of his cargo had not appeased the sea or God. Reality rushed upon him without pity, and he wanted to scream in the agony of his soul.

On the aft deck at that moment, Pasher was at the helm. Old Coos and another seaman named Proctus, experts in splicing rope, were at the bow replacing a frayed section of cable for the sea anchor when they saw the mountainous rogue wave forming like a monster out of the mist. Roaring, it bore down on the ship. Pasher screamed his warning, but he may as well have whispered. Coos and Proctus, having seen it anyway, stood for a second transfixed. Never in all his years at sea had the old sailor seen such a wave. And now his years were surely over. The wave towered closer, a wall of green water. They sucked in their breath and held on.

The ship pitched upward; then, incredibly, she soared up, up—as though she would lift from the water and fly. But before she could top the foaming crest, water surged over her deck. At the top of the wave, the full force of the gale hit her with a shriek; a roller wave caught the port quarter; and the ship lurched and started to roll, spilling the water to starboard.

The few men on top held their breath—they were capsizing for sure! The yardarm tore loose from its rear lashing to swing lazily around and dip its starboard end, furled sail and all, into the ocean. There the ship stopped, with her starboard rail barely above water—rolling no further, but unable to right herself as long as the yardarm weighted them so heavily to starboard. In this perilous position they sank into the next trough.

By then the terrified passengers and crew, thinking the ship was going over, were climbing out of the forward hatchway. Hit by the wind on the slanting deck, some fell; others crawled on hands and knees toward the high rail.

Abiel was out of his cabin immediately and gasped at the scene—the cries, the sprawling bodies, the sea foaming at the starboard rail.

This time Abiel had a job for the centurion. "Use your soldiers," he shouted to him. "Use swords if you have to. Herd them up on the high side or we're going over."

Calliades at the winch had already cranked slack into the halyard. But to the anguish of the seamen clustered around the mast, the yardarm did not budge. As Abiel feared, its weight against the slanted mast had jammed it.

Rising into another wave, the rail dipped under. "We'll have to cut the collar!" Farnaces, ashen faced, looked up at the skewed yardarm some thirty feet above them. "One more big sea, and we're gone."

"Give me your knife!"

Without listening to Farnaces' surprised protests, Abiel began climbing the mast ladder with the knife clenched in his teeth. As luck would have it, when he was nearly to the yardarm, the ladder swung round so that he was on the low side of the mast. The remaining climb was the most devilishly hard task he had ever known—as gravity tugged him toward the hissing foam below, the wind snatched and clawed, and the pitching of the mast threatened to flick him into the misty void. He was trembling from head to foot when he finally reached the collar. He tried to take the knife, but was unable to control his clenched jaw. His hand pulled away from the knife, and he nearly dropped it.

On the second try, he got the knife in hand. "Fool!" he cursed himself. His arms felt so heavy he could scarcely make them work. Sobbing with rage and exhaustion, he sawed against the collar ropes. One rope parted. His chest was burning, and he could scarcely breathe. He would cut the collar, and then he would let go and fall. He would die and end the storm forever.

The second strand parted. The collar slipped loose, the halyard jerked tight, and the huge yardarm slid silently away down the mast. Abiel thought he heard a cheer from below, but it was impossible to tell.

The captain did not let go then to fall and die. If he died, he would face God with the likely deaths of two hundred seventy-five people on his soul. No, he did not want to die. Hanging on with the last of his strength, he watched the men below cutting the brail lines. Then the entire crew lifted the yardarm; tackle and all, it slid the rest of the way over the rail into the sea. Freed of its burden, the ship began to come back level. Still trembling, Abiel rested a moment on the now-vertical ladder. Slowly and carefully he descended, pausing each time a gust flattened him against the mast. Very carefully he moved, for he did not want to die.

When Abiel was back on the deck, Farnaces slapped him on the back, and that was all. Like drugged men, everyone began filing back to shelter. It had only been a preview of the real thing, a rehearsal of when they would all die—all of them, not just one man on the mast.

Abiel retreated to his cabin and, sinking down on his pallet, buried his face in his hands. Someone opened the door. He looked up resentfully and was startled to see Demaris standing there, steadying herself against the door. Her face was drawn and hollow, but Abiel still drew in his breath at the almond-shaped eyes that so easily set his soul afire. All he could manage to say was her name.

"Abiel," her voice trembled, "you shouldn't have done that. I thought I was going to see you killed before my eyes."

"If the ship had rolled . . . would have killed all of us. Now, with that yardarm gone, we might survive."

Carefully she walked over to where he sat and knelt beside him in the gloom. For a moment they simply clung to one another in silence. The ship took another wrenching plunge. Then, to Demaris' utter surprise, Abiel began to weep in great, heaving sobs. "Who am I trying to deceive?" he moaned. "We will not survive this."

"I understand why you went up the mast like that," she said. "All these people. I can't stand it, either. I can't look them in the face . . ." She began to weep also. "Oh, if I had only not obeyed Phlegon and deceived you. I feel like a murderer."

"Stop it!" After a moment Abiel regained control of himself, then looked down into her face, barely visible in the dusk. "You must not say that," he said more softly. "If you are a murderer, what does that make *me?*"

She saw the horror in his eyes and groaned, and they clung to one another again silently, desperately.

At sunset that night there was a break in the clouds; shafts of cold, menacing light lit the waves with orange-tinted foam. Then it faded into dusk and darkness. With night the wind seemed to increase even more. "It cannot possibly blow any harder," the crew had assured each other. Yet it did. The dreaded sound of waves thudding on the deck came more and more frequently. They all sat in dazed and battered shock, knowing they would die this night. Everyone agreed it was only a matter of time until another monster wave, like the one that afternoon, would finish them. Abiel could not find it in his heart to encourage anyone. The stricken captain remained in his cabin.

In the crew's quarters, the men who were supposed to be resting lay wide awake in their berths lining the walls. The lamp, suspended from a chain, swung in crazy circles, leaving a plume of smoke behind it. Outside, the wind moaned and vibrated in the night, as if the ship were surrounded by a thousand drums in continuous roll. But sometimes there would come a dreadful silence before the ship began to rise under them again. Hearts would stop, and all would wonder if it were time now to die.

With each wrenching shock, Naso would groan involuntarily, as if receiving the blow himself. They all lay spent, mouths agape and eyes wide. If water had burst in, some of them would not likely have even moved.

Plautus sat braced in a corner with a pile of hemp. Slowly, with great concentration, he was weaving cords for rope to calm himself. The others could only watch him with dumb envy.

Then into the cabin lurched Alexander. The imperial haughtiness gone, he steadied himself against the door frame while shadows from the swinging lamp, playing across his wet cheeks and hollow eyes, turned his face into a flickering skull. "The captain . . ." he said hoarsely, his voice trembling. They raised on their elbows to listen.

"The captain has panicked! He's hysterical . . . he's crying like a baby in his cabin. I just passed there and I *heard* him, I tell you!"

At their blank stares, Alexander seemed to grow angry. "He *knows* we're dead. Curse him. That Jew has finally killed us all—just like I always knew he would. He knows it himself now!"

Another tremendous shock, and they held their breaths.

"I'll tell you this now," Alexander raved on, "if this tub floats long enough to blow into shore somewhere, *I* am not going to flounder and drown like everybody else!"

They only stared uncomprehending. Finally Farnaces spoke up. "You'll sprout wings and fly?"

"The boat, fool!" said Alexander. "If this ship runs aground, we can make it ashore in the boat!"

"And leave the passengers?"

"They'll drown anyway. Let Neptune have them."

"We're not going to get that close to shore anyway," muttered Naso.

"Well, if we do," quavered Alexander, "I'm taking the boat, and anybody who will help me let it down. We'll get back at that Jew for this! He's lost his nerve . . . we're all dead! He's in there crying like a baby. Don't you hear me, you fools?"

In the dim passenger cabin, a group was clustered for comfort around Paul. To them came old Coos who, with his dark hooded cloak and toothless smile, looked the personification of death itself. "The captain, Ben Heled, wants to see you, Paul. In his cabin if you will come. He must see you."

"Now?"

"Yes. Please come," said Coos. "I will help you get there if you like."

The two old men made their way aft through the lower passageway. There remained a short run across the open deck to Abiel's cabin, so Paul pulled the hood of his wet cloak over his head. Though soaked, it at least kept the wind out of his aching ears. Coos waited until the ship sloped down a wave before they ventured across to the master's cabin, and went in.

The captain was at his table. In the box on the table normally reserved for the water pitcher was his folded prayer shawl; Paul supposed that he had been praying. In the lantern light he sat very pale. As each thudding shock went through the ship, he jerked and winced as if being flogged.

Holding to the fastened table, Paul carefully sat down across from Abiel. Coos deftly eased out the door and left them alone.

The shipmaster looked up, and his exhausted voice came barely above a whisper. "Paul?"

"What is it, Abiel?"

"Paul . . . you were once a rabbi. Is that true?"

It was hardly the question Paul had expected. "Why, yes, I was."

"Then tell me. Is it not in the law of Moses that if someone has an ox which he knew would kill a man, yet still he lets the ox run free, that the owner is responsible for any deaths his animal causes?"

"I cannot understand why you ask this, Abiel. But yes, in the second book of Moses it is written."

"Then does it mean," Abiel asked shakily, "if a man *knows* he is putting people in danger, but he does it anyway, then he is guilty if they die?"

Then Paul understood what the shipmaster was asking and perceived the agony of his soul. "You are being very honest, Ben Heled."

"But does it really mean I am guilty?"

Paul fixed the younger man directly in his gaze. "Yes."

Abiel doubled forward slightly as if in pain and groaned. "Paul, it was only that I wanted Demaris so badly! I wanted to earn her freedom and make her my wife. *Just once* I put my desires above all else, even the safety of my ship. Just once. It was such a reasonable thing . . ."

Paul nodded. "When Adam sinned at the beginning of creation, was it not also a reasonable thing? But it brought death to all mankind, just as you have brought death to this ship."

After a moment, Abiel looked up, hollowed-eyed. "Then, Paul, I am as guilty as Adam!" He held up his hands to Paul as if to display the guilt. Then he buried his face and began to weep, his shoulders shaking with great, bitter sobs. "I cannot die condemned. Paul, I cannot bear it!"

"No, you cannot," said Paul. Then the old apostle's face lit with that beguiling, lovely smile. "But Abiel, look at me! Listen. You cannot bear your sin. But there is One who can!"

Abiel looked into Paul's face. "I think I know of whom you speak."

"Yes. He of whom it was written so long ago . . ." Slowly Paul quoted once more, softly, those precious words given to Isaiah the prophet—words which have survived and towered over the ashes of history: "He was wounded for our transgressions, He was bruised for our iniquities: the chastisement of our peace was upon Him; and with His stripes we are healed. All we like sheep have gone astray; we have turned every one to his own way; and the Lord hath laid on Him the iniquity of us all."

"*My* iniquity . . . on the Nazarene?" said Abiel.

"Yes."

Then, with a sudden rush, Abiel saw, and the light of understanding dawned on his face. "The crucified man of whom David wrote . . . was the Nazarene."

"Yes," said Paul. "And all the temple sacrifices we Jews have made throughout history all point toward the one great sacrifice of Messiah Himself. Abiel! If God Himself died to bear your sins, would He condemn you?"

There was a smoothing of Abiel's lined, tormented features. Almost a smile.

"Abiel," Paul urged, "do you believe Jesus is the Messiah?"

For a moment Abiel—whose own righteousness had been blown to bits in the storm—stared as if in a trance. Within his heart he felt a curious, irresistible urging. "I have cursed Him, Paul," he murmured. "I have refused to believe Him. Yet I realize it now—that I knew all along. Somehow in my heart I knew long ago who He was."

"Then will you surrender to Him? Let Him bear your sins?"

"*I will.*" And with these two words, the urging in his heart dissolved into a joyous release as the risen Messiah entered the life of Abiel Ben Heled.

Paul smiled. "And you should know, Abiel, a few moments ago Demaris and many others did the same as you."

And then, for the first time in many days, Abiel smiled.

Outside, the waves still pounded. The ship could yet splinter and wrench open at any moment. The fear and horror for the lives of his innocent passengers gripped him yet. But something had changed. He could not fully understand what had happened, even though he and Paul talked for a long time afterward. But he did know that the oppressive, choking guilt was gone. He would face God innocent of sin! How unbelievable that, even here, he could know such grateful joy.

Later that night, as he stood at the helm it occurred to Abiel that God was no longer the faraway, unreachable star, but was closer than his breath. And Abiel's voice rumbled in the wind as, amid the horrifying waves, he sang the song of the Day of Atonement, which he at last understood: "Though your sins be as scarlet, they shall be as white as snow; though they be red like crimson, they shall be as wool."

CHAPTER 14

*A*ND SO THE ARMS OF THE CROSS stretch from one end of time to the other," said Robert Bonn. "For thousands of years the Jewish prophets looked ahead to it, and for two thousand years we have looked back."

"I just never knew of it like that," Karen said. "I mean, what Paul believed and what you believe hasn't changed at all in two thousand years."

"Not a bit."

"And I always thought it was all just something Billy Graham, or somebody, invented." She laughed a little nervously and tossed her head so that her long hair, bleached from a summer of Mediterranean sun, rippled in the light.

Outside of Fabio's storage shed, the wind had risen remarkably, and puffing gusts punched the sides of the shed, rattling the tin. They listened to it a moment.

"And so they had given up hope of survival?" Karen murmured.

"Yes. And I think it's significant that it was only after they had given up, Paul told them they would live." Bonn grinned as he found the twentieth verse of the storm chapter and began to read:

> When neither sun nor stars appeared for many days and the storm continued raging, we finally gave up all hope of being saved.
> After the men had gone a long time without food, Paul stood up before them and said: "Men, you should have

taken my advice not to sail from Crete; then you would
have spared yourselves this damage and loss. But now I
urge you to keep up your courage, because not one of
you will be lost; only the ship will be destroyed. Last
night an angel of the God whose I am and whom I serve
stood beside me and said, 'Do not be afraid, Paul. You
must stand trial before Caesar; and God has graciously
given you the lives of all who sail with you.' So keep up
your courage, men, for I have faith in God that it will
happen just as He told me. Nevertheless, we must run
aground on some island."

"Now *that* is hard to imagine," Karen cut in. "I mean, here is
Paul just getting right up and saying . . ." her voice lowered
dramatically, "now listen to me fellows. *God* has just told
me . . ."

They both laughed.

"But I think," said Robert, "after the way Paul had been right
in his first prediction, it was probably the most natural thing
in the world."

"Maybe. I *can* imagine how relieved they must have been—
and grateful." She listened for a moment to the wind. "Pathet-
ically grateful."

"Yeah," said Robert, "especially after two weeks of that
pounding."

"Two weeks!"

"That's what it says in verse twenty-seven here." He began
to read again:

On the fourteenth night we were still being driven
across the Adriatic Sea, when about midnight the
sailors sensed they were approaching land. They took
soundings and found that the water was a hundred and
twenty feet deep. A short time later they took soundings again and found it was ninety feet deep. Fearing
that we would be dashed against the rocks, they
dropped four anchors from the stern and prayed for
daylight. In an attempt to escape from the ship, the
sailors let the lifeboat down into the sea, pretending
they were going to lower some anchors from the bow.

Then Paul said to the centurion and the soldiers, "Unless these men stay with the ship, you cannot be saved." So the soldiers cut the ropes that held the lifeboat and let it fall away.

"It sounds as if that last night was a hectic one," said Karen. "And after two weeks? They were probably all walking around like zombies."

"It also sounds as if Paul had pretty well taken charge of things," murmured Robert. "I suppose we should point that out to Professor Healey."

Karen's head tilted up then on a sudden impulse. "Bob, let's walk out to where we can overlook the beach."

"What?" Bonn gestured toward the rattle of rain against the shed. But then he saw the light of discovery in her eyes, and he understood. "Okay. You're crazy, but okay." He reached for the outdoor light switch.

"Leave the lights off," said Karen. "There will be enough coming from the shed."

He nodded. They walked out into the wind and the intermittent bursts of rain. Fabio's yard ended on a low bluff above the beach. The thin soil of Malta had long ago blown away from this point, and they stood on the bare limestone looking out toward the dark, pounding surf.

"It's uncanny," Karen said at last. "Way out there where we found the anchor could be the very place, you know? It's almost as if they are out there now. The ship is straining at the anchor lines; you can see their lamps flickering and hear their shouts blowing in on the wind."

Bonn felt the hair rise on the back of his neck.

Lydas Phlegon was furious. Groggy and dismayed, the merchant found Abiel as he made his way among the crew's lanterns, checking the drift lines. It was obvious, even with four anchors down, that the ship was drifting slowly toward land and jagged destruction. The captain was praying for dawn.

"Ben Heled," Lydas grabbed Abiel by the arm. "How close will we be to shore when we run aground?"

"What?" The shipmaster's voice was trembling. Ever since they had neared land, his quivering stomach had cut his voice into tremors, which he was powerless to stop. "I can't see in the dark, Lydas! I have no idea."

"Well, how do you intend to get my money ashore?"

"Your money. You're worried about your money."

"Of course I'm worried about my money! You fools cut the boat loose. How will we get my pouch ashore?"

Abiel eyed the merchant with blank weariness. "Tell you what, Lydas. In a few minutes I plan to call everyone into my cabin who has valuables in the strongbox. I will return everything to its owner. You will get your pouch then, and what happens to it will be your worry."

Phlegon swore in dismay.

At the distress on the merchant's face, Abiel paused with a sudden idea. "On second thought," he said slowly, "perhaps we should arrange something for you. Meet me in my cabin in a few minutes, will you?"

When Phlegon weaved into the captain's cabin a few minutes later, he was surprised to see not only Ben Heled, but also, slumped at the the table, a very drained centurion. Like everyone else, the Roman had lost a great deal of weight. His eyes were hollow as he sat up; he seemed past caring.

Abiel waved Phlegon to a chair. "I asked the centurion to be present," he said, "to witness any agreement we may make."

"Agreement? What are you talking about?"

"Well, as I said, I will you give you your pouch, and getting it ashore is your problem. But . . ." Abiel paused a moment, "when this ship runs aground, the water will be considerably over your head, Lydas. Depending on the shoreline, you could have a very long swim, and that pouch is heavy."

"That is precisely what I am trying to tell you!"

"Precisely. Now, I am a very strong swimmer, myself. What if I were willing to personally guarantee that your money reaches safety?"

"Ah." A sardonic grin crossed Lydas' face. "At last I understand your tender concern, Ben Heled. And what do you want in return?"

"In return, you give me Demaris."

Phlegon's eyes widened incredulously. "By the gods, Ben Heled, you *are* insane!" He coughed and wiped his mouth. "Since this vat of yours will not reach Rome, I have already lost a great deal of money. I intend to salvage at least part of it by selling Demaris in Rome—assuming we ever get there. She will bring a good price."

Abiel's heart sank. He swallowed and tried to steady his voice. "Lydas, you will lose even more if your silver goes to the bottom."

Phlegon glared suddenly at the centurion. "Do you hear this attempt at *extortion?*"

"Everyone works better with an incentive," growled the Roman.

Phlegon cursed bitterly. "You are asking more than I can afford to give you, Captain. Hades will give up the dead first! Give me the pouch, and I'll be gone."

"Alexander must get his receipts in order first. I will call you in a moment with the others. But think it over, Lydas."

"There is nothing to think over." Rising to his feet, Phlegon staggered with a lurch of the ship out into the darkness.

Abiel sighed deeply. "It was worth a try," he murmured more to himself than to Julius. "I have lost all else."

The centurion cast a wry, sidewise glance at Abiel. "Then again, perhaps God will smile on you, and Phlegon will drown. Then whose would the woman be?"

"No, no. Paul has already given us the promise of Jesus, the Christos. No one will die. God forgive me if I wished otherwise."

"Ben Heled . . . ? You *have* changed, haven't you? Along with your friend Demaris and many others!" The centurion eyed Abiel with an intense, disturbing gaze. "Ben Heled, do I understand you correctly? You have accepted . . . forgiveness . . . from this Jesus?"

Though his heart was wrenching in disappointment, Abiel managed a weak smile. "Yes, I have."

"But have you made him your *Lord* as well?"

The captain was a bit perplexed over this. "Why, of course I have made Him my Lord. He would not have the power to forgive sins unless He were God. And if God . . . of course He is Lord!"

The centurion seemed stricken.

"I've found what I have searched for all my life," Abiel went on softly. "I wish, sir, you could know Him, too."

With that, the two men looked at one another, astounded. "Since when do you care for the happiness of a Roman?" Julius murmured.

Abiel shook his head. "I almost cannot understand it myself."

The centurion passed a hand over his haggard face. "And yet, when I see the change in you, Captain, it reinforces my caution in making the same decision as you. You see, I cannot make *anyone* lord above my emperor. Not when I must do my duty if this ship runs aground in the morning." He swore softly. "And I am ill, Ben Heled."

"I don't understand," said Abiel.

"Captain, are you aware the prisoners' chains are all missing? All of them. I removed their chains so they could help throw the cargo out, many days ago. Now the chains are gone—nowhere to be found."

Anger born of exhaustion began to rise in Abiel at this seemingly pointless discourse. "We are trying to keep this ship in one piece until morning, and you concern yourself with some cursed chains?"

The centurion's voice hardened. "Captain, don't you realize that if I cannot keep my prisoners secure . . . if I cannot keep them from swimming away during the wreck . . . I must *execute* them?"

The sudden cold horror that gripped Abiel was made worse when he saw in the centurion's eyes the same horror. The shipmaster's voice was barely audible. "Not Paul! You couldn't. Not when Paul has said we will all live. Don't you know by now he speaks from God?"

"And don't you see that, under the law, I cannot be judge of guilt or innocence? If I spare one, I must spare them all. If I execute one, I must execute them all."

"Not Paul! Not on my ship!"

"On this ship or anywhere else in the empire! But save your anger for yourself, Captain. You got us into this. And now, if you can get us safely to shore so we can keep our prisoners securely, Paul and the rest will live. So it is really up to *you*." The centurion got up then to go out into the writhing gloom and mist.

After that, the night took on an aura of unreality. Abiel's young faith, which had already withstood much, now wavered for the first time. Forcing himself to think, he summoned Alexander who, after the affair with the ship's boat, seemed for once in his life to be genuinely humble.

"Get your list of passengers who have valuables in the strongbox," Abiel said curtly. "Find each one and tell him we will try to land the ship at daybreak; after that, I cannot guarantee that their things will be safe. Tell them to come in with their receipts and claim their possessions now."

When Alexander had gone to fetch the owners, Abiel, still trembling, gathered up some of his own things in a leather pouch. Strange to think that this little room, his home for the past four years, would soon be destroyed. His treasured copy of *The Coast Pilot* by Scylax the Younger went into the sack, along with his Scripture boxes and wrist straps. At the sight of these prayer artifacts, Abiel sank to his knees at the table. "Oh Lord Jesus, Messiah. I have believed in You! I have trusted Your promises to Paul that we would all be saved from the sea. O Lord, do not let Your promises be false!"

Shortly afterward the passengers filed into the cabin, holding to the walls to steady themselves. After so many endless days of storm, there was something final about this moment which drove home the fact that the end of their ordeal was near—one way or another. As he handed the jewelry and currency to their owners, the best Abiel could manage was a weak smile and a vague apology to each. Phlegon took his pouch and stalked out without a word.

At the end of the line were several prisoners under guard, retrieving the valuables which, in the end, might do them no good. At the sight of them, Abiel's spirit plummeted. There was nothing he could say to them. On their faces was the ashen threat of death; the steel of the Roman swords, real and terrible, awaited them. Abiel could not look at them. He would not let those faces burn into his memory where they would surely remain.

At last, in the early morning, Abiel went to the women's passenger area and asked for Demaris. Not caring now about convention or what anyone might think, he gently drew her to him as they stood in the passageway in their wet clothes. For a long moment he held her tightly and kissed her, thrilling at her soft warmth. "Oh that we could blink our eyes," he murmured, "and find ourselves somewhere, married and alone." Slowly he tilted her chin upward and studied the lovely face that had brought him to this moment and to the loss of everything he owned.

"Abiel," she whispered. "Oh, that the storm would not end—and I would never see the day I must go with Phlegon to Rome."

Abiel groaned inwardly. "I promise you, Demaris, one day very soon I will find you again and buy your freedom."

In exhaustion of body and spirit they clung together silently, both of them realizing he soon would have nothing with which to buy anything. Finally he stepped back from her and reached down to an object lying at his feet. "Here. I want to give this to you."

"What?"

"It's an empty wineskin. I've blown it full of air and sealed it, see? Now hang on to this. Tomorrow, when we abandon ship, you can loop your arm through the handle, and it will buoy you up until you reach shore."

She wiped her eyes, then examined the skin with a fleeting smile. "When I was a little girl in Caesarea, I used to play with these things at the seashore. But I can swim very well without it, Abiel."

"No matter how well you can swim, use it. Because if we run aground, as Paul says we will, I may not be around to look after you."

Something in his voice made her look up in questioning alarm. "Abiel?"

Grimly he told her then of the possibility that Julius might kill the prisoners.

"No," she breathed. "Not Paul!"

"Him as well. Julius doesn't want to do it, but he has killed many people before. He could do it easily." Abiel's voice hardened. "But I promise you he will not kill Paul. If I have to shield him with my own body, I'll do it."

Her eyes were wide in the lamplight. "You can't fight all of them. You'll be killed!"

"That is very possible."

"But Paul has promised—*God* has promised—none of us will die!"

"I know that. But just the same . . ."

"Abiel, don't doubt Messiah." Releasing her hold on the wall, she held to him. "Oh, Abiel, we've lost everything. But haven't we both found the most valuable thing in the world? Haven't we found the *Savior?*"

"Yes." Abiel swallowed. "But things are happening so fast. What if something goes wrong?"

CHAPTER 15

GRAY, BLEAK DAWN came at last, and with it a cold, driving rain. The crew in their soaked oiled mantles and hoods stood at the bow rail watching the rising and falling panorama before them. They all shivered from the cold and tension. The uncontrollable trembling of Abiel's stomach had worsened so that he stood slightly bent forward as if in pain. All eyes bored through the writhing, ghostly sheets of mist and rain.

"Does anybody recognize where we are?" Julius asked tightly.

They shook their heads. How could anyone know where on earth they were?

Just then the rainy curtain parted, and—"Look!"—Calliades pointed over Abiel's shoulder off the starboard quarter. Along the wooded shoreline they saw it unmistakably—a small natural bay where a creek emptied into the sea. At its mouth there appeared to be reeds and, further down toward the sea, the yellow of beach sand. "Oh," Calliades let out his breath in a long sigh. "Beautiful beach! Skipper, we can run her right into the sand there and get these people in spitting distance of shallow water!"

As Abiel watched their haven appear and reappear behind the blowing curtains of rain, the trembling of his stomach eased slightly and hope flickered. Was this how Messiah would keep his promise?

Nothing could keep the passengers below deck now. Hearing the ship was soon to be beached, they poured out into the rain carrying bedrolls and belongings. Only the prisoners remained below. Abiel sent his officers throughout the crowd to give instructions: when the ship began to move, everyone must be sitting down or braced against something solid. "Because when we hit the sand, there will be quite a jolt. Then we will let down the ladders from the bow so you can get off. If we get close enough, the water will hardly be over your heads."

Abiel found Demaris to be sure she understood. Then he headed below to see the centurion. He must be absolutely sure this nervous Roman grasped what was going to happen. In the passenger cabin he found where the soldiers had run a rope through the neckring of each prisoner and fastened it to the bulkheads, so that the prisoners were kept helplessly in line. Paul, quite calm, was near the middle.

In a cold rage, Abiel turned to the centurion. "There is no *need* for this! Your prisoners will be able to step off into the sand. We found a beach up ahead; didn't you see it?"

"This is only in case of the worst, Ben Heled." The centurion's haggard face looked worse than his prisoners'. "And do you think we will be able to escort them off?"

"Yes! Don't kill anyone. There is no need."

"I will take care of my duty, Captain. Be sure you take care of yours and get us ashore."

Another glance at Paul, and the cold anger pulsed again in Abiel. The finger he jabbed in the centurion's face could have been a dagger. "And Julius," he breathed, "let nothing happen to Paul."

"Don't threaten me, Jew. Not in front of my men. It's the worst thing you could do."

Back on the aft deck, a trembling Abiel gave what would be his last orders of the voyage. He called up the men from the bilge station and let the pump stop. Calliades, chattering with nerves and exhaustion, took the bars in hand while the rudders were lowered into the water. Then, at Abiel's signal, the seamen began hoisting the foresail to the wind. Immediately it snapped out into a billowing cloud, becoming hard to hoist fully. They watched the sail apprehensively, fearing it might split at any moment. Simultaneously they cut the anchor lines, and the ship began to move. Calliades felt once more the pressure of water against the rudders.

Faster they moved, and yet faster. Calliades would not have thought they could get such speed from just the foresail, flying full now over the bow. Of course, the wind was nearly at gale strength. Instead of tossing helplessly now, the ship planed up the backsides of the waves and flopped over them like a playful porpoise—her last gesture of defiance at the sea that had so cruelly battered her. Moment by moment the land drew closer and more distinct. In an illusion of the morning light, the beach seemed to glow like gold against the black sky.

Calliades felt *Athelia's* responsiveness as he steered. This wonderful ship! How she obeyed his commands even though he, a traitor, was taking her to her death.

Abiel at first thought it was only the rain on the rugged face of his sailmaster; then he realized that Calliades was weeping. "Here," he said. "Let me take her in. It should be by my hand."

"No, no. My job," Calliades growled. "But those lookouts had best point me to a soft place for her."

At that moment there were sudden faint screams from the lookouts at the bow, and frantic gestures to steer starboard. Snapping alert, Calliades leaned to the bars. But before the bow began to swing, as the *Athelia* was rising into a wave, they felt a sudden shock that staggered them. The prow had brushed over something very solid—a sandbar or reef. Then the bow began its plunge. Abiel stood frozen. He would remember this moment forever: the passengers, white-faced, looking up toward him, and Calliades behind him pleading "No! No!" They were still four hundred feet from shore.

Then she struck down on the reef. In his frozen surprise, Abiel had forgotten to brace himself, and the shock sent him falling forward. Had it not been for the railing, he would have been thrown down to the deck below. With the shock, a grinding, splintering rumble mingled with the screams of the passengers. The foresail yardarm kicked up, and the sail burst into streaming ribbons. Four hundred feet from land! Welling in Abiel's soul was a scream of denial. Messiah had failed! God had not kept His promise.

Even with the roar of wind and surf, there seemed to be a shocked silence. The motion of the ship was now completely changed. She had lodged on a breakwater, and the first huge wave broke against her stern with a roar. White, frenzied water burst skyward like steam from a volcano, and mist from the eruption enveloped the stern like smoke as *Athelia* shuddered and reeled.

The next few moments were a blur for Abiel. When all is lost, a man may try to salvage at least one thing. Ignoring the growing chorus of shouts around him, he stumbled down the deck stairs to the passageway and began running toward the bow—to the passenger cabin and Paul. He could hear water roaring into the hold below and was aware he could be caught and drowned before reaching the forward passageway.

With relief he saw the light dimly ahead. He turned up toward the passenger cabin door—and froze with horror. Returning from the deck were the centurion and his assistant, Gaius, silhouetted in the forward hatchway. Gaius had his sword drawn and, beside him, the centurion dragged against the passageway like a dazed man. "Ben Heled!" he croaked. "By the gods, what did we hit? There is no way we can guard the prisoners from out here!"

"Hurry, sir!" Gaius urged.

Julius released the catch on his scabbard, then saw that Abiel was not moving from in front of the cabin door. "Out of the way, Captain!" he rasped.

"Not on my ship! You'll murder no one aboard this ship!"

There came a loud cracking from the stern, and more screams from passengers on the deck above. Then, from the corner of his eye, Abiel saw Gaius' fist coming in a right hook. Rolling away from the punch, he lunged into the centurion, sending him crashing against the passage wall; the two began wrestling furiously. If he could just get the sword! If he could just get the centurion's sword!

Abiel tried to spin the smaller man toward Gaius, but the centurion was stronger than he looked, and Abiel felt a crack like lightning in his skull as the soldier struck him from behind with the hilt of his sword. In the brief second of darkness, his knees turned to rubber. Quite suddenly he was down, his back against the passageway, with Gaius' sword at his throat.

"Hold!" the centurion gasped to his optio. White-faced and breathing heavily, Julius glared down at Abiel. "Do not follow us in there or try to interfere, or we will kill you." Then the two Romans went inside to where the other soldiers waited with the prisoners.

Abiel rose slowly to his feet, trembling in pain and horror. The passenger cabin would soon be a slaughterhouse, and there was nothing he could do. . . . Then he remembered the belaying spikes back in his cabin, and a surge of energy swept through him. The perfect weapon against a sword! He would die fighting Romans, just as he had always known he might.

In a daze of fury he pushed back toward the stern through the throng of frantic humanity. Already his cabin was knee deep in water, but he waded in, surprised at how warm the water felt, in contrast to the wind and rain. Inside, all was dark. With the floor slanted crazily, the cabin seemed a foreign place, no longer his. Frantically he felt in the corner, took one of the hefty spikes in hand, and turned to the cabin door. Water was pouring into the cabin now. Wading against it with much difficulty, Abiel pulled himself out, only to be swept up by a waist-deep current of water rushing toward the passageway—now a huge, sucking drain. Utterly surprised that he could not help himself, he dropped the spike and, grabbing with both hands to the hatch frame, held on against the rushing water.

Looking up at that moment he saw a sight he would never forget. The bow had risen toward the dark sky like a great wounded whale. Clinging to rails and stanchions, or jumping into the sea, were the terrified humans who had trusted Abiel Ben Heled with their lives. He heard their cries and knew those same shrieks were even now echoing through the passenger cabin. All was death. All was death and darkness. And then the passageway dipped beneath the water.

It was ridiculous, but Abiel could not move against the inrushing water. Grimly he held on as his lungs began to burn and ache. Soon it seemed as though they would burst. He knew then that he would die. He had been deceived He had trusted a god who was not God after all, and now he would die along with his ship—along with Demaris and Paul.

A roaring filled Abiel's ears. And at that moment, from somewhere down in the holds below, a huge bubble of air burst up through the hatchway. It blew Abiel, dazed and gasping, to the surface. Instinctively he began to tread water. And as he drew in the priceless air of life in great gulps, a wave spun him out and away from the ship.

When the centurion and the optio entered the darkened cabin, everyone knew the Roman verdict—more from Julius' face than his drawn sword. Battered into submission by the storm and by fate, the prisoners stared hollow-eyed at the swords, their mouths agape. A few chattered in fear. Others pleaded. They would not try to escape—they could not. "Please! I won't! I'll give you money. I'll give you anything!" But Paul only watched the face of Julius, his eyes not leaving the centurion's.

The soldiers looked to their leader. "Give us the order, sir," said Gaius. "We must hurry!"

"Wait," said Julius. "I . . . I must be the first." He advanced toward Paul, his heart pounding while a wave of nausea swept over him. If he could just execute this man Paul and get it over, the rest would be easy. Then he and his soldiers could escape this cursed ship. But he knew, for the rest of his life, he would see the face of this gentle, good man upturned to him now without a trace of fear. "Paul," he choked. "I'm sorry. Your God has failed you. He is to blame."

"Then kill me for *your* god," said Paul, "whoever he is." The apostle's eyes flashed. "Before you kill me, Julius, tell me his name!"

"You *know* his name." Julius' back straightened. "The majesty . . . the emperor of Rome."

". . . who deserted you in Caesarea and took away your honor—the most precious thing you had. Will you kill me for *him?"*

And Paul's eyes continued to hold the centurion's as the Roman leveled his sword at the apostle's heart. Then the blade began to waver . . .

"Over here, Skipper!"

Abiel heard the voice of Calliades behind him. Woodenly he propelled himself around to see the sailmaster clinging to the looped handle of an upturned wine jar, its rounded bottom floating out of the water like a green bubble. His head pounding from the Roman blow, Abiel swam with ebbing strength to the makeshift life buoy and hooked his arm through the handle opposite Calliades. Then, too exhausted and breathless to even speak, he hung on as it carried them up and over a wave.

"By Cybele!" said Calliades. "When you went under with the stern I thought you were a dead man, Abiel. Hang on."

"Yes. Yes, thank you," Abiel gasped. Once past the reef, where swells were breaking against the grounded ship, the waves smoothed out and became much smaller. With his head higher above the surface now, Abiel could see that the water was alive with people clinging to enough debris to float an army—planks and wooden blocks, barrels, and everywhere the upturned wine jars, which had bobbed to the surface like bubbles from the torn hull.

"People are making it!" Abiel gasped. "We all could have made it—Paul, and all of them." Vainly Abiel craned his neck looking for the other most precious life aboard, but Demaris was nowhere to be seen.

As they swept past the bow, it towered darkly above them and groaned like a living thing with each swell that slammed into the stern. "Come on, swim!" urged Calliades. "Let's get past before she rolls on us."

With Calliades' sudden vigorous kicking, the jar spun slowly around. Barely ten feet behind them, Abiel saw Lydas

Phlegon trying desperately to swim while clutching his money pouch under one arm. Phlegon's mouth and nose dipped just below the surface. A desperate lunge and he rose briefly, only to sink again, his hair waving on the surface like a patch of black seaweed. A wave swept over him, and Abiel thought that if he did not release the money, he was surely gone. But Lydas emerged and lunged upward once more, his nose barely clearing the surface. In his terrified eyes was a silent scream for help.

"Let go of the pouch, fool!" Abiel barely had the strength to shout. But Phlegon, if he heard, gave no sign of it as, struggling, he dipped under again.

"Come on, we'll have to get him," Abiel gasped to Calliades.

"Let the idiot drown! We'll all drown if the hull rolls on us."

"Can't. Can't," puffed Abiel.

Calliades began to cry in frustration, cursing with each kick as they maneuvered their life buoy back toward the merchant. No sooner had they come within arm's length than he grabbed the handle Abiel was clinging to and pulled his head out of the water, his mouth agape and coughing. With the additional weight of Lydas and his money, the jar did not now provide enough lift, and both Abiel and Calliades had to kick vigorously to keep the three of them afloat.

"Drop the pouch, Lydas!" Abiel rasped. But Phlegon, his eyes bulging like a madman's, clung to the handle with a frenzied grip and shook his head. Abiel had not the strength to struggle with him. Desperately the three kicked and swam, riding the waves that swept them toward the beach. Abiel's legs felt like lead. His lungs burned and ached so that he had not even the breath to curse Lydas.

Just as Abiel was about to let go and swim on his own, while they were still fifty feet from shore, a wave let them down onto solid sand. They lifted and bumped down again. Soon the water was shallow enough to release the jar. Falling and struggling through the breaking waves, they stumbled up onto the beach, Phlegon still clutching his pouch of money. Then they sprawled down onto the sand in the cold rain, their chests heaving. After a moment, Calliades and Phlegon began crying in gratitude that, for the first time in two weeks, they were on something solid and safe.

Abiel, lying on the sand, felt the darkness creeping over him. His body, aware now that it was all over, was trying to give up and rest. But Abiel fought sleep. There was more to be done; he was the captain, after all. Slowly he rolled over in the wet sand and sat up, his head sagging between his knees. Then, with great effort, he raised his head to view the scene before him.

They were coming—lines of people emerging through the surf, falling and clinging together while the debris and jars they had used piled up on the sand. Abiel watched them, not fully comprehending what he was seeing. Two Roman soldiers, in blue tunics without their armor, crawled up onto the sand. And there was Paul with Lucanus the physician. Paul! How strange that Paul, who was dead, should be emerging from the sea as though from his grave. Further down the beach, he saw Demaris. Only then did he struggle to his feet.

"Ben Heled!" Phlegon, sitting up now with black wet hair strung across his face, glared at Abiel. "Go on to your woman friend, Ben Heled, but remember she is my slave. We made no agreement. I did not ask you to help me. Do you hear me? *I did not ask your help.*"

Abiel was numb, unable to feel anger, dismay—anything. He only stared at Phlegon a moment with eyes half closed and jaw slack. Then he turned and stumbled toward Demaris. In her wet tunic with wet hair streaming down her shoulders, she was a vision of white against the darkness of sky and sea. Abiel could see nothing else.

As he embraced her, it finally came to him that they were safe—really *safe* on land. Paul was alive; and so, it seemed, were most of his passengers. Messiah was true. Messiah was faithful! As he clung to her, his tears were of joy, yet mingled with bitterness at the realization she could soon be gone.

CHAPTER 16

*O*NCE SAFELY ON SHORE, we found out that the island was called Malta. The islanders showed us unusual kindness. They built a fire and welcomed us all because it was raining and cold. Paul gathered a pile of brushwood and, as he put it on the fire, a viper, driven out by the heat, fastened itself on his hand. When the islanders saw the snake hanging from his hand, they said to each other, "This man must be a murderer; for though he escaped from the sea, Justice has not allowed him to live." But Paul shook the snake off into the fire and suffered no ill effects. The people expected him to swell up or suddenly fall over dead, but after waiting a long time and seeing nothing unusual happen to him, they changed their minds and said he was a god.

There was an estate nearby that belonged to Publius, the chief official of the island. He welcomed us to his home and for three days entertained us hospitably. His father was sick in bed, suffering from fever and dysentery. Paul went in to see him and, after prayer, placed his hands on him and healed him. When this had happened, the rest of the sick on the island came and were cured. They honored us in many ways and when we were ready to sail, they furnished us with the supplies we needed.

It was appropriate, the islanders agreed, that the celebrations should be held in honor of those who had been rescued from the sea—those who had brought to their island Paul, the man who had shown them God. Publius was happy to entertain with yet another banquet, especially after the wonderful healing of his father. It was at this banquet that the centurion rose to make a statement.

"We Romans," he said, "have conquered the world, and all of us share in the benefits of our rule. But we conquered by shedding much blood. It may seem strange to say, then, that I have joined the kingdom of One who conquered by shedding not the blood of others, but His own I have chosen to follow Jesus, the Christos. I wish to announce it publicly. I made this decision in an instant, in the twinkling of an eye, during a moment of stress in the shipwreck. Because of that, I did not kill my prisoners as I had planned—one of whom is Paul."

Sudden murmurs ran around the tables, then quieted. "So," Julius went on, "already I owe much to my Lord, Jesus, the Christos. I look forward to learning more about Him." Looking to Abiel, he nodded. "Captain, I, too, join those who are saying that in the wreck we lost much, but gained much more. And I thank you, Ben Heled and Paul, my brothers."

For many days afterward, debris from the wreck washed ashore. Most of it was useless, except for some well-made barrels and several hundred wine jars which, having been left in the hull for ballast during the storm, eventually bobbed to the surface and washed ashore. Abiel and his crew collected these and sold them on the island for several hundred denarii. Abiel distributed the money to his crewmen in an effort to compensate them for the wages they would never receive.

After this, there was nothing more to do, and Abiel soon fell into a deep depression. The realization of what had happened to him sank home at last, and he spent too much time simply lying on his cot and looking at the ceiling. As often as Phlegon would let her, Demaris would visit him, and they would walk together in Publius' gardens or on the beach. Discussions of the future were touchy at best.

Finally, one day, Abiel went to Paul. "Paul," he moaned, "I love Demaris more than my own life. Now that we both know Jesus, Messiah—we are joined in spirit. Oh that we could be joined as well as husband and wife, and have children whom we would teach to know Him. Yet . . . I have no money with which to buy her from Phlegon. I haven't an obol to my name."

Paul cleared his throat thoughtfully. "What *are* your plans, Abiel?"

The captain rubbed a hand over his eyes. "I've thought of so many insane schemes, I've lost track of them. But . . . there is a ship wintering in port now, the *Ariel*, which is going back to Alexandria as soon as the weather is safe this spring. I've signed on as a 'proreus.' When I get back to Alexandria, I will see if my father will loan me the money to purchase Demaris. Then I'll hurry back to Rome, to buy her from whoever her owner will be after Phlegon sells her." Abiel sighed. "But we both know there are a hundred things that could go wrong. She could simply disappear in Rome, and I would never find her again. If only there was some way I could buy her from Phlegon before we leave Malta this spring!"

Paul thought for a moment. "Abiel, have you asked the Lord to make a way if it is His will for you to have her?"

Abiel was embarrassed. How impertinent, he thought, to approach the Almighty who had made Mount Sinai smoke and tremble with such a personal request a procuring a wife. "He . . . He would not understand, Paul."

Paul raised his eyebrows. "He who lived as a man for thirty-three years would not understand?" The apostle laughed warmly. "Abiel! Jesus knows you more intimately than you know yourself, and He now stands as your eternal High Priest, interceding for you before the very throne of God! Go boldly to the Throne of Grace then and make your requests known. After all, did He not answer your prayer and save all of your passengers?"

Abiel nodded.

"Then, let's ask Him now." Before Abiel could say anything, Paul took both of his hands and began to pray, warmly and earnestly. And as he prayed, Abiel knew once more that assurance that had come when he first acknowledged Jesus as Messiah—that the Master of the Universe was intimately near, even within his own spirit. He left that day with a lightened heart.

Paul, as usual, was not content only to pray, but put some action into the matter. With the centurion he visited Phlegon and pleaded with the merchant on behalf of Abiel, asking him to extend terms. But Phlegon was adamant in his refusal. Even when Publius offered to post surety for Demaris, Phlegon refused.

One day, in a private moment, he told Abiel why. "Do you remember that night aboard your ship when you humiliated me in front of those other passengers? You left bruises on my neck . . ." Lydas grew angrier as he continued. "No one gets away with that. No one. You men with your muscular bodies—you think your strength makes you better than others. Well, now we will see who is the more powerful."

Abiel, with great effort, contained his anger. "Even when I saved your life and your money both?"

"Nonsense! You have no proof I wouldn't have made it on my own. Don't flatter yourself."

Calliades, when he heard of it, was enraged. "Wasn't I right?" he roared. "Wasn't I right? You should have listened to me, Skipper, and let the jackal drown!"

> After three months we put out to sea in a ship that had wintered in the island. It was an Alexandrian ship with the figurehead of the twin gods Castor and Pollux.

For many days the island had been their haven and home. But at last, though, the day drew near when the *Castor and Pollux* would sail for Rome and the *Ariel* for Alexandria. One warm afternoon in early spring they sat on the beach, looking out at where the *Athelia* had come to ruin. All that was visible now was the top of her mast protruding from the water at a crazy angle, and in front of that the bowsprit with tattered pieces of the foresail fluttering. The sun was low, casting an orange path across the water, and in that light the bowsprit formed the dark silhouette of a cross.

"Isn't it the most amazing thing?" Demaris asked softly.

"What is amazing, Demaris?"

"That such an ugly, horrible thing as a cross should come to mean life to us."

"And so it is!" Abiel murmured, looking at her in some surprise.

She wrinkled her nose. "Oh, you Jewish men. You all think women have no understanding of deeper things."

"Hmm," Abiel smiled. "That may be one of our failings."

"You were probably surprised that Messiah would redeem a woman."

Abiel turned her face toward his. "But I am so glad He did!"

"Not nearly as glad as I am. And I am so glad we can be joined in Him one day," she said wistfully. "And we will have children who will know Him, too."

The low sun had turned their world to a mellow gold, and he looked at her face—dusky and glowing, slightly upturned with that undaunted spirit he had seen in the storm. He wanted her more than life itself. After a moment, though, her wistful smile faded, and she began poking a stick into the sand at her feet.

"Abiel, you will leave for Alexandria soon, won't you?"

"I didn't want to talk about that. But we will probably leave on the same day you leave for Rome on the *Castor*. Both captains are watching each other's judgment of the weather."

"Abiel," her voice began to tremble, "look at what I have cost you! And then, when you finally come to Rome to buy my freedom, I will cost you even more."

"Demaris, I want to hear no more of that . . ."

"No. Now you listen to me! We have both prayed and prayed, and we have asked our Lord to make a way for you to have me. And the Lord has not answered! What if it isn't His will? I mean," she wiped her eyes, "why doesn't He make an easier way?"

Abiel thought a moment and looked at the silhouetted cross. "I have asked myself the same question." Abiel murmured softly. "But when Messiah came to purchase our souls and redeem us, He did not make an easy way for himself. He paid for us with the dearest thing He had. How dare I ask Him to make an easy way for me?"

He tipped her chin up, as usual, to look into her blue eyes. "And, my love, when I purchase you at a dear price, will you not be all the more precious to me?"

On impulse she kissed him and they melted in each other's embrace for a long moment. "I love you, Abiel," she whispered. "Oh, has there ever been a man like you? How did I ever merit the love of such a one?"

"Now, you have the address of my father's house in Alexandria," Abiel said after a moment. "And I've told Julius how to leave your whereabouts on file with the Maritime Steward's office. So, when I come to Rome, I will be able to find you, Demaris. Sooner than you think, I will return and buy your freedom."

Abiel spoke with confidence. He did not know of the devastation soon to come to Alexandria's Jews with the war that would soon erupt between Judea and Rome. And Demaris did not know of the terrible things that would be done to Christians in Rome under Nero. But both knew of the hundred other things which could go wrong. For the rest of that golden evening, they tried to dismiss such thoughts from mind.

The night before they were to leave the island, Abiel and Demaris met once more. She wore her hair in a plaited garland as it had been the first day he had seen her in Myra an eternity ago. They rejoiced and tried not to weep. She strummed the lyre and, with an occasional tremor in her voice, sang softly to him a Jewish song:

> The Lord bless you and keep you;
> The Lord make his face shine upon you,
> And be gracious to you·
> The Lord lift up his countenance upon you,
> And give you peace.

By morning the storm was blowing in earnest as rain lashed the windows of Fabio's house. But a cheery fire blazed in the stone hearth, reflecting in the plates lining the cedar panels of the dining room. When Karen appeared for breakfast, Cal eyed her mischievously. "Well, where were *you* last night?"

Fabio's old housekeeper fussed over her immediately. "I see your bed empty, and I worry for you."

"Well, for the information of you *all*," Karen said flippantly, "Robert and I spent a long time out there with our anchor last night, didn't we, Bob? We practically relived the voyage of our ship—and the wreck too."

There was something different about the girl. They all noticed it, but couldn't pinpoint just what. A softening of the face? Her assertive edginess perhaps not so abrasive? She seemed almost happy.

"Bob should be a novelist," Karen went on. "He imagined a lot of different things which could have happened on the ship with Paul and the centurion, you know? And we wondered a lot about the shipmaster—whether or not he found salvation. . . ."

"Found salvation?" Healey looked up quizzically. "That's an odd phrase for you, Karen."

"Well," she seemed suddenly a bit embarrassed. "Robert and I talked about a lot of things which I never understood before, when we were wondering about the Jewish shipmaster. We speculated if he found happiness . . ."

"Happiness?" Healey snorted. "I doubt it. I imagine happiness was just as hard to find then as it is now—as elusive as that ship is proving to be."

The night passed for Abiel in sleepless distress. The next morning, as he packed the few belongings given him by the islanders, a knock at the door startled him. Resentfully he opened it to see Calliades, Naso, Coos, Plautus, Farnaces, and most of his old crew standing in the shaded entrance—those who were going with him back to Alexandria. "You're early, aren't you?" Abiel snapped.

"Not at all!" Calliades said heartily. "If anything, we're late, skipper! We should have done this a month ago. Come on in, my fellows!"

"Calliades, what are you men doing?" Abiel growled. He was literally brushed aside as his crew crowded into the small apartment. "Have you been drinking?"

"Oh, a little," said Calliades. "Here, skipper. The fellows and I have thrown our purses together and bought a little gift for you." On his signal the room fell quiet, and Calliades handed Abiel a scroll of heavy parchment.

"What is this?"

"Why don't you read it and find out?"

While they watched him, Abiel unrolled the scroll and read quickly, but it took a moment to read down through the legal jargon—and for it all to register. What he held in his hands was a bill of sale, attested by Publius with his official seal and signed by Lydas Phlegon. The merchandise described was the slave, Demaris of Caesarea, sold to the magister navis Abiel Ben Heled of Alexandria. Price: five hundred denarii, commercial standard.

Abiel's eyes grew wide.

"Paul has said he will perform your betrothal before his ship sails," said Coos slyly.

Abiel stared at the parchment, hardly daring to believe. It was as if he were again sitting exhausted on the sand, watching in a daze as his passengers and Paul emerged alive from the sea. He sank onto the edge of his bed and read the scroll again before looking up at them all. "How?" he croaked.

Calliades shrugged. "The money you gave us, skipper, for the wine jars. Plus we chipped in some more of what these islanders gave us. So . . . we figured five hundred denarii would buy a good slave."

"And Phlegon agreed to sell her for that?"

They shuffled a bit, embarrassed. "Well, we had to use some persuasion on him," said Farnaces at last. "It was the centurion's idea to do it; but he couldn't do it himself, being a Roman officer and all . . ."

"But us crazy sailors," Calliades winked, "there is no telling what we might do on a dark night to somebody we don't like."

Suddenly Abiel grinned widely and shook his head. "Calliades, how can I ever repay you all?"

"The fun I had "persuading" Phlegon last night is all the payment I want, skipper. I've been wanting to do that a long time. So . . . what are you waiting for? Go and get her. She's waiting for you."

Still a bit dazed, Abiel started out almost drunkenly. But before long he broke into a stride; then a run.

"Happiness?" said Healey again. "Well, I'll tell you what, Bonn. If you're so concerned about your shipmaster, and if you're so sure there's going to be a heaven, why don't you look him up when you get there? Ask him."

Bonn grinned. "A good suggestion, sir. I'll do that."

"And guess what?" The happiness played about Karen's face again. "So will I."

CHRISTIAN HERALD ASSOCIATION AND ITS MINISTRIES

CHRISTIAN HERALD ASSOCIATION, founded in 1878, publishes The Christian Herald Magazine, one of the leading interdenominational religious monthlies in America. Through its wide circulation, it brings inspiring articles and the latest news of religious developments to many families. From the magazine's pages came the initiative for CHRISTIAN HERALD CHILDREN and THE BOWERY MISSION, two individually supported not-for-profit corporations.

CHRISTIAN HERALD CHILDREN, established in 1894, is the name for a unique and dynamic ministry to disadvantaged children, offering hope and opportunities which would not otherwise be available for reasons of poverty and neglect. The goal is to develop each child's potential and to demonstrate Christian compassion and understanding to children in need.

Mont Lawn is a permanent camp located in Bushkill, Pennsylvania. It is the focal point of a ministry which provides a healthful "vacation with a purpose" to children who without it would be confined to the streets of the city. Up to 1000 children between the age of 7 and 11 come to Mont Lawn each year.

Christian Herald Children maintains year-round contact with children by means of a *City Youth Ministry*. Central to its philosophy is the belief that only through sustained relationships and demonstrated concern can individual lives be truly enriched. Special emphasis is on individual guidance, spiritual and family counseling and tutoring. This follow-up ministry to inner-city children culminates for many in financial assistance toward higher education and career counseling.

THE BOWERY MISSION, located at 227 Bowery, New York City, has since 1879 been reaching out to the lost men on the Bowery, offering them what could be their last chance to rebuild their lives. Every man is fed, clothed and ministered to. Countless numbers have entered the 90-day residential rehabilitation program at the Bowery Mission. A concentrated ministry of counseling, medical care, nutrition therapy, Bible study and Gospel services awakens a man to spiritual renewal within himself.

These ministries are supported solely by the voluntary contributions of individuals and by legacies and bequests. Contributions are tax deductible. Checks should be made out either to CHRISTIAN HERALD CHILDREN or to THE BOWERY MISSION.

Administrative Office: 40 Overlook Drive, Chappaqua, New York 10514
Telephone: (914) 769-9000